Death By Chocolate
A Josiah Reynolds Mystery

Abigail Keam

Worker Bee Press

ISBN 978 0 9893745 5 2

9 15

Published in the USA by

Worker Bee Press
P.O. Box 485
Nicholasville, KY 40340

Abigail Keam

Acknowledgements

The author wishes to thank Al's Bar, which consented to be used as a drinking hole for my poetry-writing cop, Kelly, and Morris Book Shop. www.morrisbookshop.com

Thanks to my editor, Patti DeYoung.

Thanks to the Lexington Farmers' Market, www.lexingtonfarmersmarket.com

Artwork by Cricket Press www.cricket-press.com

Book jacket by Peter Keam
Author's photograph by Peter Keam

By The Same Author

Death By A HoneyBee I
Death By Drowning II
Death By Bridle III
Death By Bourbon IV
Death By Lotto V
Death By Chocolate VI
Death By Haunting VII
Death By Derby VIII

The Princess Maura Fantasy Series

Wall Of Doom I
Wall Of Peril II
Wall Of Glory III
Wall Of Conquest IV

Last Chance For Love Romance Series

Last Chance Motel I
Gasping For Air II
The Siren's Call

To John and Bunny,
who bought my first book.

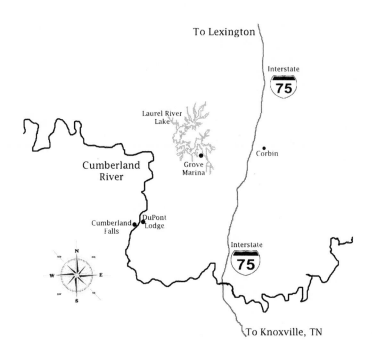

To Lexington

Interstate
75

Laurel River Lake

Cumberland River

Grove Marina

Corbin

Cumberland Falls

DuPont Lodge

Interstate
75

To Knoxville, TN

Preface

Walter Neff was nursing a drink at Al's Bar on the corner of Sixth and Limestone. He intended to do more than nurse it. He intended to get stinking drunk.

Neff was bitter. He was bitter because he had been cheated out of millions by a dame he liked. It was hard to lose the money, but the money and the woman both? It made him feel like a chump. Neff hated to come up empty.

His mind raced with a thousand schemes. The money was lost, but maybe he could still have the dame. It was worth a shot.

Anger and jealousy gnawed at him. He knew deep in his heart that the woman was out of his reach.

Neff slammed the bar countertop in frustration with his fist.

"Whoa there, partner," drawled a handsome blond-haired man. He looked like Tab Hunter. "Got problems?"

"None of your business, *pard-nar*," sneered Neff.

"That's where you're wrong."

Neff swiveled to get a good look at his companion. "What makes you say so?"

"I would say that we have mutual friends. Perhaps mutual experiences as well?"

"Sure we do, buddy." Neff turned back on his stool and took another sip of his drink.

The blond man leaned in closer. "I'm very serious. I'm always serious with people who have been burned by a certain redhead."

Neff faced the younger man and wavered for a moment. "Okay. I'll throw caution to the wind. What's your pitch?"

"I know that a woman with red hair and green eyes cost you millions of dollars. Money that is now being wasted on Lexington's terminally down and out."

"How do you know that?"

"I make it my business to know. Let's just say I've had previous experiences with the lady in question."

Neff squinted while tapping his forehead. His mind was fuzzy, but still worked when he concentrated. "I know who you are. You're that loser that went crazy and tried to . . ."

"If I'm a loser, so are you. Perhaps you would like to discuss how to become a winner. You know, revenge is a dish best served cold. I have a plan that will serve it on a platter. Would you like to hear it?"

Neff hesitated for a moment, but his anger was stronger than his common sense. "Let's talk where there ain't so many ears."

"That's all right with me. By the way, my name is O'nan. Fred O'nan."

Neff shook his hand. "I have the feeling that this is the beginning of a beautiful friendship."

"So do I," cooed O'nan, studying Neff like a wildcat does a careless rabbit. "So do I."

Prologue

In a corner booth at Al's Bar sat a young woman with short ash blond hair. She was preening in a compact mirror while powdering her nose, which drew attention from the gadget resembling a smart phone recording O'nan and Neff.

When O'nan and Neff left the bar together, the woman nodded to two men sitting at the bar.

Taking their cue, they sauntered out into the street and followed the pair.

Another man immediately scooted into the booth with the woman. "Put eyes and ears in both their apartments. I want each room available. Make sure you tag their cars as well," she ordered.

"Sure thing, Asa. Cars are already booted," he said in a thick Cockney accent.

Asa frowned at the use of her name. Her tone turned very chilly. "I want their every movement tracked."

Getting the message, the man reminded her, "This is gonna cost a bundle."

"Don't worry about the money. I'll take care of everyone. Just do your best."

"Yes, ma'am."

"You've seen O'nan's psychological profile. If it were your mother, what would you do?"

"He would already have been neutralized. Made it look like a car accident, ma'am."

Asa nodded in agreement. She wasn't ruling that option out.

She threw a twenty on the table and left with her employee.

Outside they parted.

Asa got into a black SUV with government tags and pulled off her wig. "Take me home," she said to the driver.

"To the airport?"

"Sorry, no. Take me home to the Butterfly. I need to see my mother."

Before the SUV could take off, the back door was wrenched open.

"What are you doing, Asa?" asked Officer Kelly, leaning in. "I was sitting in the back watching you watching O'nan. Don't do anything stupid. The city would love to see your mother trip up so they don't have to pay her the rest of the settlement. And don't think they don't know you're here. There were three other cops at Al's Bar tonight."

"I must be getting sloppy," admitted Asa. She smiled sweetly at him.

Kelly's eyes grew soft. "Asa. Asa."

Asa leaned forward and kissed Kelly, holding onto him tightly.

He passionately returned her kiss, winding his arms about her. Asa pulled Kelly into the back seat and mouthed to her driver–"GO!"

"Where're we going?" asked a bewildered Kelly.

"Shut up," replied Asa tenderly. "Just shut up and kiss me."

1

Linc and I were hulling black walnuts for a wedding cake when someone began banging on the front door and ringing the doorbell.

My heart jumped into my throat. I told Linc to take Baby to my bedroom and lock the steel door. He was not to come out until his grandmother, Eunice, told him it was okay.

Linc, thrilled at the prospect of danger, did what he was told with relish.

Baby, thrilled at the prospect of being with Linc, did what the boy commanded and followed happily, especially when Linc promised a treat.

Turning my attention to the front door, I watched Eunice hurry to the security monitors. In addition to the monitors, I had had several panic buttons installed in the house and was sitting next to one, ready to press it, when

Eunice exclaimed, "Why it's Ginny Wheelwright! She looks fit to be tied. You want me to tell her you're home?"

"She must have news about her boy," I replied. "Let her in, by all means."

Eunice had barely opened the steel double door when Ginny barged passed her.

"Josiah. Josiah!" she called, looking in the kitchen.

"I'm over here."

Ginny looked a mess. Her face was blotchy and her one good eye was red from crying. To make her look totally alien, her glass eye had flipped over, showing only the gold side, but then would flip again when she twitched.

I guess my face showed astonishment at her appearance.

"I know I look awful. Can't help that."

"Ginny. They've found Dwight's body?"

"If only. That would give me some peace on the matter. Oh, Josiah. That wife of his has petitioned to have Dwight declared dead."

"You have to be missing seven years in order to be declared dead."

"That's what I thought, but if she can prove extenuating circumstances, then the courts will give an earlier approval."

"What's the rush? Dwight's only been missing five months. Give the detectives a little longer to work the case. Dwight might be stumbling around somewhere with amnesia. It's been known to happen."

"That's what I said, but she said she wanted to get on with her life."

"Her childhood sweetheart goes missing for only five months and she wants to forget him so soon?"

"My sentiments, exactly. I think it's awfully cold."

"What else did she say?"

"She told me to mind my own business." Ginny began crying again. "My son is my business. Where is he, Josiah? Where can my baby be?"

Ginny blew her nose with a used tissue and then continued lamenting, "And that business partner of his, Farley Webb, has moved all of Dwight's things out of his office. He just packed them up and took Dwight's things over to Selena. Then she took his things to Goodwill. It's like they both are trying to erase my boy."

Eunice brought a tray of coffee, tea, cookies, and a fresh box of tissues. Then she discreetly vamoosed into my bedroom with Linc, giving Ginny some privacy.

I'm not a touchy-feely person. I'm not given to hugs or kisses, but I did reach out and pat Ginny's hand.

Ginny grabbed it and tugged. "Ya gotta help me, Jo. The investigation's going nowhere."

Shaking my head, I said, "NOOO! I'm not going to get involved with issues like this anymore."

"This isn't some issue. This is my boy who used to play with your girl right there on that patio. You babysat him. You cooked for him."

I tried to pull away.

15

"When Asa went to trial, who was there for you? Me. When Brannon left, so did most of your friends, but I stuck by you. Now it's payback time. You gotta help me."

Jumping Jehosaphat!

Why did I have to stick my hand out to her?

I was in no shape physically or emotionally to solve another mystery. That's what police and shamuses were for. I should have thrown Ginny out right then and there.

Instead, I asked, "What do you want me to do?"

2

My name is Josiah Reynolds.

I've worked hard all my life. I was a tenured art history professor at the University of Kentucky until I took up beekeeping. It wasn't that I wanted to retire from teaching. I loved it, but my personal life got in the way.

Mainly I was chased out by the constant gossiping in the office after my husband left me for a younger woman and colleagues stabbing me in the back when I was a candidate for the Department Chair's position.

I hate office politics. Good riddance was what I said as I turned in my resignation. I didn't have to put up with those jerks' smug knowing looks or cruel remarks– just loud enough for me to hear. Screw them!

Bees are how I make my living now . . . if that is what you can call it. They are much more civil creatures. The honeybees just want to collect their nectar. They don't have a backstory. They don't bring baggage to work. Their only agenda is to make lovely golden honey.

Every Saturday, I sell their honey at the Farmers' Market.

I have other sources of income. I rent out my house, the Butterfly, for tours and weddings, which makes a tidy little profit for me now. I also board horses, mainly racing Thoroughbreds. That money goes back into the farm.

My vices are flower arrangements, having my hair done every so often, and my animals. I love animals. I have sheep, chickens, a couple of goats, llamas, peacocks, two rescue racehorses, numerous barn cats, and one mangy lazy slobbery English Mastiff named Baby.

I live in a large iconic house called the Butterfly because its second roof looks like wings from a distance.

It is a modern-style house that was an experiment in complete sustainable living from the cradle-to-the-grave. There are no steps in the house and the hallways are extremely wide.

The entire back of the house is bulletproof glass overlooking the Kentucky River. The bulletproof glass was installed to protect the residents, mainly me, from stray bullets shot across the Kentucky River by drunken deer hunters.

The house sits on a cliff overlooking the Kentucky River. This area is called the Palisades, which is one of the most fragile and sensitive environments in the world.

I do everything I can to protect it, but it seems everyone from developers to the Kentucky Department of Transportation wants to destroy one of the great wonders of the world.

Greedy moneymen can't wait to get their hands on a failing horse farm so they can turn it into a tacky little subdivision. It's like the devil is pushing folks out of one of the last paradises on earth so another strip mall can be built.

Speaking of the devil, last year I had an accident. Accident–hell! I was thrown off the cliff at my house by a cop who hated me. Anyway, that's another story.

While I recovered in Key West, my daughter, Asa, along with my best friend, Matt, had the entire estate upgraded. Things had gotten a little shabby after my husband left and took our money with him. I guess he figured that if he had already stabbed me, he might as well gut me, too. That's in the figurative sense.

Anyway, he died of a heart attack leaving me with nothing but a headache.

His girlfriend, Ellen Boudreaux, thinks their child should have some sort of legal interest in the Butterfly, as it was Brannon's masterpiece.

Actually, it was my idea and design. He just built it. His specialty was the restoration of antebellum homes.

I guess Ellen thinks that since she got my money, some of my couture dresses, and my best jewelry, she should have the roof over my head as well. She threatens all the time to take me to court. "Well, get on with it, girl" is what I say.

But I don't want to talk about Brannon. I get riled up just thinking about him. It was with our daughter, Asa, that I currently was having a hissy fit. We were having a discussion in the great room. No, it was more like an argument.

"You simply must not see Kelly anymore," I demanded.

"I don't think that is going to happen, Mother."

I held out my hands. "Asa, he has a wife and two young children to consider. He loves his wife."

"He loves me too."

"If you loved Kelly, you would not make him choose between you and his family. You could have had him, but you left him high and dry after high school without even saying goodbye. Since then he has made a life and you shouldn't break that up."

"So, because I made a mistake when I was young, I should suffer the rest of my life? He should suffer?"

"There are other people to consider now."

"Lots of people get divorced who have children and they get on with their lives."

"But Kelly is happily married. There is no reason for a divorce."

"He will be happily divorced then."

"Oh, Asa, how can you be so selfish? Really. This is not a game."

"I've done nothing but sacrifice my whole life. I had a career, but that was taken from me. I did the right thing, but got hammered for it. Now I want what I want. I'm tired of being left empty-handed."

"If you force Kelly to forsake his family, he will eventually resent you. After the thrill of being with you wears off, he will feel guilty and go home. You will be heartbroken and alone. This is not right for either of you. No happiness will come from this."

"What about your affair with Jake? He was married," retorted Asa.

"That was not the same thing at all. Jake didn't know he was still married. He thought he was divorced and, Miss Know-It-All, his wife had been cheating on him. He wanted a divorce."

I was getting angry because hearing Jake's name made me sad. "Don't bring up Jake. You don't know what you're talking about, but look at what happened. As soon as his wife got sick, he ran home. Both Jake and Kelly are honorable men, and they will do the honorable thing in the long run."

"I'll take my chances," spat out Asa.

She could be such a little cuss. "You're so stubborn."

"But you still love me?"

"Just because I love you doesn't mean I have to approve of your behavior. I'm very sorry to say this, but you're acting just like your father," I accused.

I could see that made Asa blanch.

"That's not fair, Mother."

"It's accurate. You watch Kelly with his family. See if I'm not right. He loves his wife. Yes. Yes. Yes. I know that you are the love of his life, but he still loves his wife and his children. They are his life now, Asa."

"Ah, crap. Why does everything have to be so complicated?"

"My advice to you is to clean up this relationship with Kelly. Give it an ending. Tell him that you'll always love him, but that nothing can come of it."

"I'll think on it."

"You do that."

"By the way, he's coming over for dinner."

"Oh, for goodness sake, Asa."

"He doesn't know that I told you about our . . . relationship. As far as you know, he's just a friend coming over to see us both."

"Asa, you really take the cake."

My daughter gave me a willful grin. "You can pump him for information about Dwight Wheelwright."

"Okay, but no hanky-panky. I have to look his wife in the face."

"I promise."

"You'll study on what I said?" I begged.

"I'll bend my mind around it."

"Ain't fittin'. Ain't fittin'."

I knew that my beautiful daughter was playing with matches and she was going to set herself on fire.

3

I served poached Cumberland River rainbow trout on a bed of polenta, with side dishes of wilted spinach flavored with bacon grease, and honey-glazed carrots. Dessert was a homemade cheesecake prepared with Kentucky-made soft goat cheese with a drizzling of pureed raspberries.

"It's been a long time since I've had one of your home-cooked meals, Josiah," commented Officer Kelly.

"Thank you. Asa helped me, as I can't stand for long periods of time."

"Well, you both did a tremendous job. I'm really enjoying eating this. We usually don't have time to cook a really good meal . . . with the kids and all. It's just 'get something hot on the table that the boys will eat.' You know how it is when you're busy."

"Too bad your family is not here to join us," I said.

Asa shot me a dirty look.

"The wife took the boys to her parents for the holidays, since I had to work."

"I'm sorry to hear that," I replied, thinking Kelly had just told me a big whopper. "So that means you'll be alone for Thanksgiving?"

"I'm sorry to say I will be," Kelly gave me a big grin, "unless you give me sanctuary."

"I will always have food and a roof for my good friend and the savior of that mangy mutt who has buried his snout in your lap."

Kelly gave a loud hoot while rubbing Baby's ears.

Baby responded by swallowing a large amount of saliva as he looked up adoringly at Kelly.

Asa advised, "You can push him away. He just wants something to fall from your plate."

"That's not it. Baby knows that Kelly saved him and is giving him much deserved doggy love."

"I don't mind, Asa," assured Kelly. "I love the attention. We're old buddies, aren't we, Baby?"

Baby swallowed again, and flicked his nose with his long raspy wet tongue before licking Kelly's hands.

"Ooooh, Mother, see what Baby's done. He's got drool all over Kelly."

"Asa, it's okay," repeated Kelly, grinning. "Really."

I kind of got the idea that Kelly loved the ruckus centering on him as I rose to get a wet dish towel.

Breaking his concentration on Kelly, Baby followed me into the kitchen and then back again to the table . . . a two-hundred-pound shadow thudding behind me.

"Here you go, Kelly," I said, handing him the wet cloth. "Baby, leave Kelly alone. He's trying to eat."

Asa opened the patio door and pushed Baby out. We were finally able to enjoy our food in peace.

"Kelly, the rainbow trout was caught by Dwight Wheelwright. He always gives me about six to a dozen trout when he goes on his fishing trips. He takes several a year. I guess I should say 'gave' instead of 'gives'. Any break in the case?"

Kelly took a bite of his cheesecake before committing himself. "It's the darndest case I've ever worked on. We can't come to any conclusion. Right now, it's a cold case, as we have nothing to decide whether his disappearance was foul play, an accident, or that Dwight just walked away."

"You don't think he left town without saying a word to anyone. That doesn't seem like Dwight to leave his family high and dry."

Asa spoke up. "People do walk away from their lives all the time."

"Was something going on in Dwight's life that would make him just up and leave?"

Kelly shook his head. "We talked to dozens of people–friends, relatives and no one had a bad word to say about Dwight. Hard working. Loyal family man. Good to his mother.

"We couldn't find any evidence of gambling, bad debts, women, drinking . . . nothing. Dwight was as clean as they come. I think the most trouble he got into was several speeding tickets. He liked to put the pedal to the metal."

"Ginny told me that Dwight always goes to the Falls for a fishing trip right before his birthday. This year it was going to be special as the moonbow at Cumberland Falls was going to be visible while he was staying at Dupont Lodge," I related.

"Ever since Dwight was in high school, he always went trout fishing around his birthday. He used to go with his dad, but since his dad's passing, Dwight went by himself," related Kelly.

"The funny thing is that I ran into Dwight at a filling station several weeks before he disappeared. He told me that everything was great. His business was doing fine," Kelly continued.

"Did he mention the fishing trip?" asked Asa.

"Yep. Said he was going around the first and would be back before the third. Said fishing trips were his time to reflect. You know, get his head straight."

"Did you notice anything odd about Dwight?" I inquired.

"No. Dwight was Dwight. Happy. Bright. I never saw that guy down. The whole thing's a mess," remarked Kelly. "Asa, remember how much fun Dwight was in school?"

"Yes, he was a very pleasant boy."

"So he wasn't in debt? He had no vices that you know of?" I questioned.

Kelly took another bite of his cheesecake before confiding, "His wife, Selena, said he left early on the morning of the first to go fishing. He was to be back on the night of the third. She was planning a birthday party for him."

I nodded in agreement. "Yes, I was invited. We waited hours, but Dwight never showed. Finally Ginny called the police to file a missing person's report."

"She called the Kentucky State Police and they called the local authorities. They found Dwight's truck at the Grove Marina on Laurel River Lake. No signs of foul play. The car was locked and his wallet was in the car's glove compartment with his ID, credit cards, and two hundred dollars," related Kelly.

"And he had already checked out of the Dupont Lodge?" asked Asa while cutting another piece of cheesecake for Kelly.

"Yeah. To me it looked like he checked out, but wanted to get in a few more hours of fishing before heading home."

"I always thought he fished on the Cumberland River. I'm confused," I stated.

"The Cumberland River and Laurel River Lake are really a stone's throw from each other, but I can see where Dwight might fish on the Cumberland one day and then try his luck on the lake the next," answered Kelly, tracing a map on the table with his knife.

"Were fingerprints taken?" asked Asa while folding her napkin.

"The truck was processed, but only fingerprints of Dwight and Selena were found."

Asa interrupted, "I take it the lake was dragged."

"Don't know. The lake's awfully deep. I know they had scuba divers."

I thought for a moment. "Was the Falls' pool checked? I was thinking that perhaps he changed his mind and fished on the Cumberland River . . . fell and then was swept away by the current going over the Falls."

"An entire stretch of the Cumberland River down to the Cumberland Falls was searched, including the Falls' pool in case he had changed his location, but we are talking about two separate water systems. They found no sign of him in the Cumberland River, Laurel River or Laurel Lake," related Kelly.

"But his cap was found six weeks ago in the lake," I interjected.

"But that is the weird part, Josiah. The cap was his to be sure, but it didn't look like it had been in the water for months. There was no discoloration. No mold. It looked almost new, just wet. Some fisherman found it in the water where the lake had been searched weeks earlier."

"Do you think it was a plant?"

"Could be."

"So you privately think it was foul play?"

"I knew Dwight. You knew Dwight. Did he seem like the kind of person to leave his widowed mother, his wife, and baby girl? Not this guy."

"Yes, I've known Dwight since he was very little. I don't think he left of his own accord," I agreed. "I'll tell you another thing that bothers me is Selena's behavior. It's like she's not even grieving."

Asa asked, "What do you mean, Mom?"

"It wasn't but a few weeks after they found Dwight's hat that she wants to have a memorial for him. It would seem to me that a distraught wife would hold out for a few more months before declaring her beloved husband dead."

Asa countered, "Maybe he wasn't so beloved."

"I was thinking the same," I replied. "Have the police looked into Selena?"

"I'm not supposed to tell you this," divulged Kelly, "but Dwight had a half million dollar life insurance policy."

"The wife did it," declared Asa. She reared back in her chair with a smug smile on her face.

Kelly shook his head. "That's where this gets creepy. The beneficiaries are Dwight's mother and his daughter. His wife was not included at all."

"That's odd," I responded, watching Asa pour some port into glasses. "What does his will say?"

"There is no will. I guess Dwight thought he had plenty of time to draw up one."

"If he was far-thinking enough to buy life insurance, why didn't he have a will? It doesn't make sense." Now that I had Kelly in a talkative mood, I was going to squeeze every ounce of information out of him that I could. Yeah, I know I was taking advantage of his kind nature, but I had promised Ginny so I had to make good.

"Not having his wife's name on the life insurance policy tells me that their marriage might have had problems. That's just not normal for Dwight not to include her," professed Asa.

"That's what we thought," revealed Kelly, "but she's clean as a whistle. No one has a bad thing to say against her, except for Ginny Wheelwright."

"That doesn't mean there weren't issues. It just means Dwight and Selena kept their business at home," I stated.

I was suddenly tired. The thought of Dwight missing overwhelmed me. I was tired of death. I was tired of seeing good people get the shaft. It made me afraid. It made me angry.

Kelly and Asa began clearing the table as I lumbered off to bed, but not before I let Baby in. He was miffed that he had been put outside earlier.

"Baby, don't be mad," I whispered. "I've got treats in the bedroom for you."

Baby's ears perked up at the mention of the word "treats."

Suddenly a thought flashed in my mind and then fizzled out like a burned match. It was something important about Dwight. Realizing that I knew an important fact about Dwight, I tried, but couldn't pull it up from the depths of my subconscious.

It must have been something that I had seen or heard, but what was it?

I could only hope that it would emerge on its own. Perhaps it would be enough to set things right.

I could hope, couldn't I?

4

I moseyed over to Ginny's house and found her putting up missing person posters of Dwight several streets away.

I opened the car window and leaned over. "Ginny. It's cold out here. Let me take you home."

Determined to put up the rest of her posters, Ginny shook her head.

"Come on, Ginny. I came to talk to you about Dwight. Come on now. My leg's hurtin' awful." I always use that excuse to get people to do what I want.

People are usually more compassionate than I give them credit for. They dislike being the cause of someone else's physical pain. At least the sane people. I guess we can rule out sadists. When I run across one, I usually leave them alone. They're joy killers.

You know how I feel about suffering. I think suffering is crap and I have no use for those who like to suffer and those who like to cause suffering.

Ginny reluctantly got into the car. "Someone keeps pulling down these posters. I can't figure out who it can be."

"Probably some smart-ass teenagers," I replied. "Listen, I want to ask you some questions."

"Okay."

"Did Dwight have a life insurance policy?"

"Yes, I found out about it when the insurance company contacted me. They sent out an insurance man to talk to me personally. I had no idea before that."

"What did the insurance man say?"

"Dwight had taken out a five hundred thousand dollar life insurance policy making me and his daughter the beneficiaries."

"Doesn't it strike you odd that Selena was not named?"

"Very."

"Does Selena have money of her own?"

"No, she comes from a middle-class family. You know Dwight met her at church camp when he was sixteen. They have been thick . . . were thick as thieves ever since then."

"Ginny, you don't have to change your verb tense for me. Speak like Dwight's coming home tomorrow."

Ginny shot me a grateful look. "Selena has been getting on me for using the present tense. She says something happened to Dwight and that he's not coming home. She says me talking like that gets on her nerves."

"Don't you think that's odd, Ginny? You'd think she'd be turning the state upside down looking for Dwight."

"Jo, I'll tell ya. I never warmed up to Selena, but we were cordial with one another. I thought she was stuck-up . . . ashamed of her beginnings.

"She was constantly harping on Dwight to do better. Selena wanted a bigger house, a better car, fancy clothes. Nothing ever satisfied that girl."

"But they lived in a very expensive house and took exotic vacations. I thought Dwight's business was doing well."

"It was. It is. He and Farley had so many accounts, they had to take on more employees. But it was very stressful, you know. That's why Dwight would go fishing. Just to wind down from the office. But Selena was saying that she wanted a horse farm. Those farms cost millions of dollars. Even with the good money Dwight made, they couldn't afford a horse farm. It was ludicrous."

"So Selena doesn't have other income?" I asked. I wanted to make sure I got this information right. It never hurts to ask the same question twice to make sure you get the same answer.

"As far as I know, she doesn't. Her parents are still alive and in good health, so she won't be inheriting from them for some time, and then it will be modest."

"What was your reaction when you found out that Selena was not a beneficiary?"

"I was taken back." Ginny rubbed her good eye. "I thought it odd. Dwight was awful tired that year, especially the last month. He told me he wished Selena would get a hobby and leave him alone."

"So they were having trouble?"

"I don't know if I would call their marriage troubled, but Dwight was starting to seem perturbed about something. It could have been Selena harping all the time about money, or it could have been problems at work. Dwight was so closed-mouth. He wouldn't open up to me."

I turned into Ginny's driveway and stopped the car. "I just have a few more questions."

"Aren't you coming in, Josiah?"

"Naw. Take a rain check though. I just want to get this straight. You had no idea that Dwight had taken out a life insurance policy, let alone made you a beneficiary?"

Ginny nodded yes.

"Dwight seemed upset about something, or at least concerned, besides being tired?"

"That's right. But as far as I know, nothing could have been wrong. He could have just been exhausted from work."

"Selena has no extra income that you know of?"

"Correct."

"He and Farley got along?"

"They were best friends and good business partners. The business was flourishing."

"What happens with the business now?" I asked.

"According to their agreement, Farley can continue giving Selena her share of the profits, or he can buy her out. She has no direct say in the business. It's all in Farley's hands."

"Do you think Farley wanted the business for himself?"

Ginny shook her head. "That doesn't make sense . . . not with the business doing as well as it was. There was plenty of money for both partners. And if Farley wanted control of the business, he could have bought Dwight out."

"Would Dwight have sold?"

"Yes. Dwight would never be a partner with someone who wanted him out. That was just his nature. He didn't like conflict."

"Was there an unhappy client?"

"I don't think so. Farley and Dwight bent over backwards for their customers. They were becoming the number one PR firm in the Bluegrass area. They even had clients located in Louisville and Cincinnati. Nashville too."

"Just a few more questions."

"I'll help all I can."

"What did the insurance man say?"

"He said that until a death certificate was issued, the money would not be paid, and it usually takes seven years to declare a missing person dead. That was fine by me. I don't want to make money off my son's misfortune."

"How did Selena take it that she was not listed on the policy?"

"She's never brought it up."

"If you or I had discovered that our husbands had not listed us as beneficiaries, what would our reactions have been?"

"I would have raised holy hell."

"Exactly."

"I know for a fact that Selena had nothing to do directly with Dwight's disappearance. I was with her every day Dwight was away. We were getting the house ready for the birthday party. You know. You were at the party.

"She simply did not have time to travel all the way to Cumberland Falls and then back again," shared Ginny.

"Well, there goes that. She was my first suspect. Always start with those closest to the victim."

"You can rule her out. She didn't have the opportunity to do anything."

"Ginny, do you ever think, in your heart of hearts, that Dwight had enough and walked away?"

Ginny was thoughtful for a moment. "No, Josiah. He would never have walked away from his daughter on his own accord. Something terrible happened to my boy and I'm not going to rest until I find out the truth."

With that, Ginny shut the car door and went inside.

5

I called Detective Goetz's number and he picked up on the first ring.

"Whaddya want?"

"Most people say hello first."

"Whaddya want?"

"Do I have to want something?"

"You usually do."

"How come that's not a problem when you want something? Remember, I almost got my head bashed in helping you with a case. Remember Arthur Greene?"

"Whaddya want?" Goetz groused again.

"I want some info on Dwight Wheelwright's case."

"No can do. Still pending."

"Ah, come on. Help out a pal."

"Are you sticking your nose into it?"

"Dwight's mother is an old friend of mine and she asked me to poke around a little."

"Isn't there anyone in town who isn't an old friend of yours?"

"Just give me the skinny," I begged.

"Can't. Now don't bother me again unless it is to ask me over for a meal." Detective Goetz hung up the phone.

Jumping Jehosaphat! That didn't go well.

6

Refusing to give up, I went downtown, hoping to catch Goetz at one of his lunch haunts. I rode down Main Street and turned onto Vine. Nothing.

Then a light bulb flashed in my mind. I cut over to Jefferson Street and parked my car. Spying Goetz's car, I knew I had hit pay dirt.

Casually walking into Stella's Deli, I looked the room over. Ah ha. There he was! Drifting over to Goetz's table, I sat down.

Goetz looked up from his peanut butter and banana sandwich. His left eye twitched a bit before he spat out, "Ah, hell. How did you find me?"

"It was lunch time. Just a simple matter of deduction."

"I told you I couldn't talk about the case. It's still pending."

"You can tell me your hunches."

"But I don't want to."

"You owe me."

"No, I don't. I've saved your bacon a couple of times. You owe me."

"You're such an egotist. You've saved me once, and only because I stuck my neck out for you on one of your cases."

"Josiah, you just wear me out. You know that."

Goetz put down his sandwich and glared.

"I will make you a homemade lemon pound cake if you spill some of your expert insight into the case."

"Done."

"I knew it. You just wanted a bribe."

Goetz took a sip of his drink while looking around at the lunch crowd. Leaning over the table and in a very low voice he revealed, "I don't have a single theory of what happened. The pieces of this puzzle don't add up right."

"Meaning?"

"His truck was found. No sign of foul play, but that means nothing. Someone could have caught up with Dwight while he was fishing."

"Isn't that the working theory?"

"Not really. The police chief thinks Dwight just took a powder."

"I'm asking you what you think."

"I think someone killed Dwight and buried him somewhere in the Daniel Boone National Forest."

"For what reason?"

"'Cause they're nuts. Serial killer. A robbery that got out of hand. Who knows?"

"What about closer to home?" I asked.

"Checked that out. Nobody said anything was wrong between Dwight and his wife or any co-worker. Wheelwright didn't have an enemy in the world."

"As far as you know."

"Why do you have to make a big deal out of everything? Wheelwright was killed by an unknown person and buried in the woods. During hunting season, some slob is going to stumble across his remains. Case closed."

"What about his cap being found in Laurel Lake several weeks ago?"

Goetz reared back in his seat. "Who told you that?"

"Uhmmm. Selena," I lied. "She is going to petition the court to declare Dwight dead. I thought you had to wait seven years."

"If Mrs. Wheelwright finds a sympathetic judge and presents him with evidence of Dwight's possible demise, then she might not have to wait that long. Lots of judges think seven years is too long.

"If the court says it might grant her petition, then notices will have to be placed in all the major newspapers. If no one makes contact after a reasonable time, then a judge might declare Mr. Wheelwright dead, as every effort had been made to find him."

"What do you think about him having an accident and falling into the Cumberland River instead of the lake?"

"Unlikely. The Cumberland is not that deep."

"Wouldn't his body have popped up by now in Laurel Lake?"

"Not if the body was snagged on something in the deepest part of the lake. It would be easy to miss."

"I still don't understand why you think it is foul play."

"Because of the hat. Wheelwright's hat was almost pristine. It hadn't been in the water those five months. No discoloration. No moss or slime. I think someone planted that hat to make it look like Wheelwright had fallen in Laurel Lake."

"Like someone who was a beneficiary of a life insurance policy?"

"You think his own mother killed him?" laughed Goetz.

"NO!"

"Or maybe his five-year-old daughter?"

"Of course not."

"We checked out the wife. She's clean. You got nothing there. I'm telling you, some stranger killed Wheelwright. It's the only thing that makes sense."

"But there's no motive with that theory."

"Crazy people don't need a motive . . . because they're crazy. End of story." Goetz took a bite of his sandwich.

I grabbed the other half of it.

"Hey!" protested Goetz.

I rose with sandwich in hand. "Thanks for asking me to join you for lunch, but I gotta go." Then I picked up his glass and drank the last of his soft drink.

Goetz looked forlornly at his empty glass. "You better not forget that lemon pound cake."

"It's on my to-do list." I made my way out of the crowded deli, saying hello to a few people I knew, and walked the few feet to my car.

Before I got in, I noticed a dark blue sedan with tinted windows parked across the street. It pulled out after I passed it, followed for a couple of blocks and then turned right while I went straight. Hmmm.

7

I headed down Jefferson Street and then cut over to Second Street to see if I could catch Franklin in. I parked behind the apartment building and knocked on his back door.

Franklin was Matt's ex-boyfriend. They had split up when Matt decided to marry Meriah Caldwell, the famous mystery writer.

But the wedding didn't take place, as a distraught woman decided to murder her rival and then kill herself at the wedding.

You can see how a bride might want to postpone the blessed event. Meriah not only postponed the event, but went running back to Los Angeles. Good-bye, Kentucky!

But she went running back pregnant.

Supposedly, Matt is to assume custody of the baby when it is born. I'll believe that when I see it.

I don't know if Franklin and Matt are an item again, but Franklin is helping get ready . . . or at least accessorize for the baby.

I knocked again.

When he didn't answer, I turned the doorknob. The door opened. I stuck my head inside and called his name.

"I'm in the living room," he yelled. "Watch where you step."

Since it was hard for me to lift my feet, I had to scoot items out of my way . . . toys of every type, baby clothes, baby car seat, pieces of a crib, rocker, etc.

"What is going on?"

Franklin was seated on the floor in his living room looking bewildered at the instructions for a highchair.

"Things for the baby, of course. Hey, can you read these instructions and help me out?"

"Franklin, this is nuts. Does Matt know you have all this stuff?"

"Uhmmm, no. I got carried away, I guess," he replied, looking hopelessly at the baby merchandise engulfing the room.

I threw several teddy bears over my shoulder onto the floor, so I could sit in a chair. "You need to take most of this back. Babies don't need all of this. Give a kid a cardboard box and he is just as happy."

"What about the educational toys? The coloring books? The Legos? The hand puppets?" Franklin cradled an orangutan puppet. "The Star Trek communicator? The Star Wars light saber?"

"What does a baby need with a chemistry set?" I mused.

"I got that for me."

"Is this a Tribble?" I asked, holding a round furry stuffed toy. It started to make a noise like the Tribbles on the Star Trek episode, *The Trouble With Tribbles*. "Now this is cool. Can I have this?"

"Give me that," said Franklin, gathering up his Tribbles. "They come in a set."

"There must be thousands of dollars worth of baby things here, Franklin. Can you afford all this?"

"That's what credit cards are for," he sniffed.

"You get the receipts and I will help you take these things back. This is just too much. Matt doesn't have room for all this. A baby needs a crib, a changing table, monitor, car seat, baby bath, and a rocker. That's it–besides food, clothes, and diapers."

"What about a baby blanket?"

"Well, pick one out of the several you have purchased," I advised, holding up three different baby blankets. "And pick out a stuffed toy you would want the baby to have. Everything else should go back. Goodness, you have the baby's college fund on the floor here."

Franklin gave me a pouty face. "Okay," he said reluctantly. "I was just trying to help."

"We'll go in my car. I don't know how you managed to stuff this all into your Smart car."

Franklin looked glumly around the room. "Oh, this is several weeks worth of shopping. I simply couldn't stop myself."

I began picking up items off the floor using my cane. Many of the bags still had the receipts in them. "Let's start with these," I suggested.

As Franklin was putting bags in the back of my car, I hid a Tribble in my coat pocket. I know I can be a stinker, but why should Franklin have all the Tribbles?

Franklin came back in to get the last load of baby paraphernalia when he spied his pile of Tribbles. "You stole a Tribble," he accused. "You stole from a baby!"

"No, I stole from you," I rejoined. "Why can't I have one Tribble? You are using my gas to take this stuff back. Can I have this Tribble?"

"No, buy your own damn Tribble."

"You're going to have to wrestle me to the ground to get this Tribble back."

"Am I going to have to watch my checkbook and wallet around you, too?"

"Don't be so dramatic, Franklin. It will make up for that crystal vase you took while last at my house," I replied, following him out to the car.

Franklin stopped in his tracks and gave me a sheepish grin. "Oh, you know about that, huh?"

"Not until I saw it on your sideboard just now. I think a crystal vase out steals a Tribble." I got in and started the car while Franklin messed with his seatbelt.

"Jeez, I feel so stupid now."

"'Cause you stole my expensive vase?"

"No. Because I didn't move quick enough to hide the vase once I heard your voice."

I laughed. "You can be such a turd."

We cut through the alley onto Third Street.

Franklin was chatting about his new job when I spied a dark blue sedan with tinted windows parked on the street.

"Franklin, shut up."

"What's wrong?"

"Look in the mirror. Have you ever seen that blue sedan before?"

Franklin flipped down his sun visor and peered into the mirror. "Never seen it before. Doesn't belong to anyone that I know."

"That is the third time I've seen it."

"Coincidence."

"Maybe, but I am going to call Goetz about it."

"There's nothing he can do without a license plate number."

"Keep your eye out for it, will ya?"

"Oui, mon Capitaine."

We traveled without incident to the stores, with Franklin keeping a lookout for the blue sedan. When we were finished, I was exhausted but Franklin was several thousand dollars richer. I dropped him off and went straight home, glancing in my rear view mirror the entire trip.

Thirty minutes later, I was safely inside the Butterfly. I made sure the alarm was on before I made the call to Goetz.

I put the phone down.

I didn't want to sound like a whining alarmist to Goetz.

Maybe it was a coincidence.

Maybe I should mention it to Asa first.

Maybe I was being silly.

Maybe I was right to be suspicious.

What to do? What to do?

8

It was a packed house for Thanksgiving.

Asa, Kelly, Ginny, Matt, Shaneika, and Linc were in the great room playing Trivial Pursuit while Eunice and I prepared the Thanksgiving feast.

Matt had installed a rolling chair in the kitchen so I could sit to prepare food.

Eunice pulled pumpkin pies from the oven and placed them by the homemade Dutch apple pie, lemon meringue pie, and flourless chocolate cake.

I checked the turkey. "Eunice, see what you think. I'm afraid if we leave the turkey in any longer it will get dry."

Eunice stuck the turkey with a fork and then basted it for the millionth time. "The juices are running clear. You're right. We should take it out."

I called Matt and he came running to pull the turkey from the oven onto the counter for us.

"Sure looks good," he said, pulling a small piece off.

"We're putting vegetables in now. Can you pick up June? I'll call and let her know that you're coming so she'll be waiting outside."

"No problem. Isn't she having Thanksgiving with Charles or her nephew, Tony?"

"Charles went to see his wife's people in Charleston, South Carolina, and Tony said he'd rather stick his hand in a bucket of lye than to celebrate Thanksgiving with the Colonists, so Lady Elsmere is dining with us."

Eunice was putting in the macaroni and cheese casserole, sweet potato casserole, corn pudding, and the mashed potatoes with added cheese and sour cream into the ovens. "Don't dawdle, Matt. We'll be eating in an hour. These dishes won't take long to cook."

I checked on the greasy green beans with ham hock in the crock-pot as Matt stole another piece of turkey before leaving for the Big House, which is what we called Lady Elsmere's antebellum home.

My late husband, Brannon, had refurbished the dilapidated mansion to its former glory and then some by adding two new wings. The white stone Greek Revival mansion with its wide front portico and thirty-foot tall round columns in the front, made a lasting impression. It was a magnificent building of twenty thousand square feet in which one old lady lived—Lady Elsmere, aka June Webster from Monkey's Eyebrow, Kentucky, with her ne'er-do-well nephew Sir Anthony and his valet, Giles, who were "on the lam" from Great Britain.

Franklin and Asa set the table while Ginny, Shaneika, Kelly, and Linc had turned their attention to watching football on TV.

If there hadn't been the shadow of Dwight hanging over the festivities, it would have been a perfect day.

As it was, I wanted the day to be as nice as possible for Ginny since this was the first major holiday since Dwight's disappearance. That miserable daughter-in-law of hers didn't even invite Ginny for Thanksgiving. What a crappy thing to do.

Okay. I steal stuffed toys and lie occasionally, but I do have standards and there are some lines you just don't cross over—like leaving a grieving widow woman alone on Thanksgiving. Not unless you want her swigging vodka out of a bottle while watching the Macy's Thanksgiving Parade.

Finally!

The front door opened and in flew June, with Matt following with a case of champagne.

Oh, the day just got better.

Eunice called out, "Children, get your hands clean. Dinner will be on the table in three." She turned to Matt. "Can you carve the turkey please?"

"Sure thing. Just let me put some champagne on ice first."

I began placing bowls of food on the buffet table around a huge floral centerpiece Kelly had brought.

Smiling, I stood back and looked at the dining table. It was gorgeous, with white linen napkins and tablecloth plus the beeswax candles on it and the buffet tables.

Suddenly that little flash of an idea popped into my head again, and vanished like a puff of smoke. Darn it! Why couldn't I catch onto it? It was important. I just felt it.

Did it have to do with tables or decorations or food or gatherings? What was it?

It would drive me crazy until I could catch it.

9

Kelly put his fork down. "I can't eat another bite or I'll pop."

Matt affectionately squeezed my hand. "Josiah, you and Miss Eunice have outdone yourselves. That was a meal fit for a king." He rose from the table. "But I'm going to have a small slice of all the desserts before I call it quits."

Kelly undid his belt. "I just can't eat anymore now, but leave the desserts out. Whose knows what can happen in an hour?"

Shaneika instructed her mother to go rest. "Mom, Linc and I will clean up. You and Josiah have done enough."

"I'll help," said Asa.

"Me, too," echoed Franklin. "It's the least I can do."

June gave me a cheesy grin, while rising. "I'm going to get a bottle of champagne and watch football."

"Don't get too drunk, June. You'll fall and then sue me."

"Now that's a pleasant thought. So glad you mentioned it."

"I'm going to take a nap," I announced. "I'm beat."

Ginny followed me to my bedroom with Baby lumbering behind her. He wanted to sleep off his treats of turkey surreptitiously handed under the table.

"Jo, is something wrong?" she asked.

"There is a thought, a bit of information having to do with Dwight that won't surface. It's like I know something, but I don't know what. I can't explain it, but something keeps flashing and it's important. Stupid, I know."

"Maybe it will come to you in your dreams."

"Sure," I laughed. "Ever since the accident, my brain doesn't retrieve information like it used to. You're right. Maybe it will just float to the surface one day."

"I'm going to help clean up and then leave. Thank you for having me. I really didn't want to be alone."

Yawning, I replied, "That's what friends are for, Ginny. Make sure you take some of the leftovers home."

If Ginny replied, I didn't hear it.

I was fast asleep.

10

I sat up.

That's it!

The missing piece!

Something that had bothered me at the time, but I didn't register the significance of what I had seen.

I went out into the great room. Everyone was gone. Pulling up a chair, I sat before the floral centerpiece and contemplated.

What if Dwight had never made it to the Cumberland Falls?

What if Dwight had been killed in town and it was made to look like he had gone to the Cumberland Falls?

Clever. Clever. Clever.

11

Dwight had an excessive sweet tooth.

Every year Ginny would have a local candy store make a large milk chocolate centerpiece for Dwight's birthday instead of having a cake.

Dwight would keep it in his office and hack off pieces until it was all gone. It was his private stash.

"Ginny, do you still have the chocolate centerpiece that was at Dwight's birthday party?"

"It's in the freezer. Why?"

"I'd like to see it."

Surprise registered on Ginny's face. "Seems strange, but all right. Follow me."

I followed Ginny down into her basement where she kept a large freezer. Opening it, she pulled out a heavy object covered in tinfoil.

"It's a little messed up," Ginny babbled. "I had to retrieve it from the garbage."

"The garbage? Who put it there?"

"Beats me. I sure was mad that someone would throw away Dwight's chocolate horse centerpiece. It was expensive."

I peeled away the foil and picked up the frozen chunk of chocolate made to look like a running racehorse. "Gosh, this is really heavy. How much does it weight?"

"About twenty-three pounds. Why are you curious about the chocolate?"

"Let's get it tested."

"What for?"

"Ginny, do you remember how upset you were. Somehow the chocolate got damaged before the party. It was smudged and looked like a leg had broken off and someone had tried to repair it. It looked awful."

"I had forgotten, but I still don't see why you are interested in the centerpiece. I just assumed that my granddaughter had pulled it off the table and Selena fixed it the best she could for the party."

"Just let me have it. I'll bring it back. Promise."

"Are you going to tell me why?"

"I'd rather not until I know for sure."

Ginny wavered.

"Do you trust me or not? You asked me to help you, so don't tie my hands."

"You're right. I'm being silly. It's just a piece of chocolate, right?" Ginny wrapped the chocolate again and carried it out to my car. "Let me know something soon."

"I will as soon as I find something concrete," I replied, waving goodbye as I backed out of Ginny's driveway.

I surely hoped I was wrong about my theory.

12

"Can you tell me what the report says without all the jargon?" I asked, sitting in the lab's conference room.

"First of all, no one should eat this chocolate. It's contaminated with germs," replied the technician, glancing at the report. She closed it and pushed it toward me.

"Inside the chocolate?"

"Outside, with lots of little nasty buggers making their home."

"It was found in the trash bin."

"That would explain the salmonella found on it."

"It had been in the freezer. Wouldn't that kill bacteria?" I questioned, scanning the report.

"Not salmonella. Don't touch it without wearing gloves."

I had the sudden urge to wash my hands. "What else did you find?"

"It was hard to ascertain what you wanted since all you said was 'just find something odd about it.'"

"Did you?"

"It was in pretty bad shape when I got it. It was supposed to be a horse? Didn't look like a horse."

I was growing impatient with the lab technician. "Just the facts, ma'am."

"Oh, cute. *Dragnet.* I get it." The technician peered at the report. "I guess the most important thing is that I found specks of blood on it."

"Human blood?"

"I found both chicken and human blood. I guess the chicken blood accounts for the salmonella."

"Can the human blood be ID'd? Can you do a DNA test on it?"

"There was no request for DNA testing. I did group the blood type, though. It was O-positive. That's all I could do with it being in the shape it was."

"Don't most people have O-positive blood?"

"Thirty-seven percent have O-positive. The next largest group is A-positive." She handed me the report. "I have listed all the bacteria on this thing." She scooted the container holding the chunk of chocolate toward me.

"Nothing else odd about it?" I asked, deflated.

"I don't know what to say. We found what we could, given the parameters we were given. Except for the blood, I would say the results are normal for something

61

that had been thrown in the garbage and pulled out again. It's nasty. Get rid of it."

"I can't," I replied, frowning. "It might be the clue to finding a missing man."

The technician shuddered as she handed me the bill. "Pay on the way out, please. Is there anything else?"

I shook my head. Looking at the bill, I swallowed. It was substantial. I sure hope Ginny would reimburse me as it was going to really impact my grocery money. But I would tell her about the report later . . . after I did some more snooping . . . I mean, investigating.

13

There are rules about solving a murder.

Rule 1: Always start with the person closest to the victim.

Rule 2: If that person is cleared, go on to the next closest person, and so on and so on.

Rule 3: Alcohol and drugs fuel most murders. The perpetrator never would have caused harm if sober.

Rule 4: Once mind-altering agents are ruled out, murder is about sex, money or power, unless the murderer is a psycho. Find the motive and you will discover the killer.

Rule 5: There is always an unknown factor.

Rule 6: No matter how well one has planned a murder or how much one hates the victim, it is hard to kill someone. That's why so many mistakes are made during a killing. It messes with the murderer's mind.

Somewhere hardwired into our DNA, we know it's very, very, very wrong to kill a human being. Again, that is if you're not a psycho.

However, after meeting so many jackasses during my fifty-one years of living, I'm surprised more people aren't knocked-off. They simply wear you down with their meanness, carelessness or stupidity until you simply can't take it anymore.

Sometimes when I read the paper and see who has been shot, blown-up or hit in back of the head with a greasy skillet, I think the world has been done a favor.

Think I'm a little jaded? Gee, what gave you that idea? I'm not the only one who delighted in some people's passing.

Irvin S. Cobb, a humorist from Paducah, Kentucky, said of someone, "I have just heard of his illness. Let's hope it's nothing trivial."

Our seventh president, Andrew Jackson supposedly said on his deathbed, "My only regrets are that I did not hang (John C.) Calhoun and shoot (Henry) Clay."

Last but not least, Mark Twain is known for saying about the death of an acquaintance, "I didn't attend the funeral, but I sent a nice letter saying I approved of it."

But Dwight Wheelwright wasn't taking up space. He was a good man who loved his family, worked very hard, took care of his widowed mother, paid his taxes and went to church. He drank only socially, went to Keeneland for the races twice a year, liked fishing and was twenty pounds overweight, but who isn't. He smoked a cigar when offered one, but never developed a habit for cigarettes.

He was very knowledgeable about tools. In fact, I still use several birdhouses I bought from Dwight that he had made in his high school shop class. He was bright, but not super bright. Just a nice Joe, who would ask you if you needed help as you were miserably trying to change a flat tire.

So where was I on my investigation?

I ruled out Ginny—as few mothers murder their sons—even though she would gain financially from his death. I believed her when she said she hadn't known about the life insurance policy. Besides, she was too weak and had that glass eye, which would have popped out at the most inopportune time. Naw, Ginny couldn't have done it.

Alrighty then. Let's go to the next one in line for the money—Dwight's daughter. Ruled her out immediately. Most five-year-olds don't even know what money is. It's just ridiculous to think a five-year-old had anything to do with this. I crossed her name off my list.

That left Selena. Selena. Selena. Selena.

Now I had lots of things written on my yellow notepad about Selena.

1. Selena seemed in a hurry to put Dwight's disappearance behind her.
2. Selena was angry that Ginny was still putting up missing person posters about Dwight.
3. Selena was jumping the gun in having Dwight declared legally dead.

But all this information had come from Ginny, who could have been biased. I needed to see for myself if Selena was really trying to discard the love of her life with nary a tear.

I thought I'd go pay a visit. You know—pay my respects. I'd think of something to get into the house.

I usually do.

14

I was trying to hold my cane and balance a casserole dish while reaching for the doorbell. Not an easy feat. I waited and waited and waited until I took my cane and hit the front door with annoying repetition. I hope Selena wasn't taking a nap.

"Mrs. Reynolds?"

I snapped my head toward the driveway. There stood Selena, looking flummoxed and pulling off a pair of work gloves. I flashed a smile and held out my best microwaveable Pyrex dish. "Hello, Selena. I've brought you a casserole."

She didn't move forward to take it, but eyed me suspiciously as though I were a Greek bearing gifts. So I had to resort to my trump card. "Dear, my leg hurts. Do you think I could sit down somewhere?"

I was sitting in Selena's kitchen sipping a cup of tea while watching her put the casserole in the freezer. She then joined me at the kitchen table.

"What's all this?" I asked, looking at a mound of snapshots stacked on the table.

Selena smiled. "These are our vacation pictures. I was trying to organize them so I could put them in a proper album. 'Trying' is the operative word. It's taking me a long time. When I pick up a picture, it reminds me of all the good times Dwight and I used to have, and then I just get lost in time. I look up and an hour has gone by with me just remembering." She pulled the pictures into a stack. "I'll get it done sooner or later. It's hard to go through them. You know what I mean?"

"I certainly do," I replied. "I know what it means to lose a husband."

"That's right. You're a widow too. I had forgotten."

"What makes you think you're one? Dwight's body has never been found. He could be alive."

Selena's eyes teared up. She pressed her hand to her heart. "I would feel it here if he was alive. He never would have left the baby or me. No one will ever convince me that he left us except by death. No one!"

I looked around for a tissue box. Seeing none, I handed her my lace handkerchief.

Selena gratefully accepted it, dabbing at her eyes.

"You know that Ginny feels differently. She clings to a sliver of hope that Dwight might still be alive. Maybe that's not a bad idea . . . to have hope like that, I mean."

Selena expelled a long, exasperated sigh. "Mrs. Reynolds. I think Ginny needs professional help."

"She says that you get upset when she puts up posters about Dwight. Even if he is dead, what harm can those posters pose?"

"Because I see them everywhere I go and so does my daughter, who cries when she sees her daddy's face. It's upsetting to us both to be constantly reminded of our loss. But no matter how I explain the situation to her, she will not stop begging for him. It's very cruel what Ginny does."

"I guess Ginny feels that unless she has a body to grieve over that Dwight is not really dead. Surely you can understand that?"

"I do, but she refuses to see my point of view. I've got a little girl who's mourning the loss of her daddy to worry about. That's my main priority now."

There was nothing about what Selena was saying with which I could disagree. There were pictures of Dwight and Selena's wedding on the living room walls, and his clothes still hung in their bedroom closet. I know because I peeked when I said I was using the bathroom. Maybe Ginny was wrong about Selena. It seemed to me that Selena was just trying to cope with a terrible situation the best way she knew how.

Selena was moving away from the pain.

I knew about this type of pain and sympathized.

It was still hard for me, and Brannon had been gone for years now.

The pain of loss never leaves. You just learn how to live with it, that's all.

15

"I can't believe that she snookered you, Josiah. You're usually more perceptive."

"I'm telling you what I saw. There were pictures of Dwight on the wall, his clothes were still in the closet, and Selena seemed genuinely traumatized. I think she believes she is doing what is in the best interest of her child."

"Pshaw," snorted Ginny.

I laid my hand on Ginny's arm. "Ginny, you might have to accept that Dwight is dead. Or at least, stop looking for him. It's tearing the rest of your family apart at a time when you and Selena should be a comfort to each other."

Ginny glared steadily at me with her good eye. "Piss off, Josiah!"

16

"She actually told you to piss off?" laughed Lady Elsmere, clasping her hands in glee.

"Can you believe that? After all that trouble I went to."

"No good deed goes unpunished," murmured Charles.

"Thank you, Charles," I said, reaching for a bourbon neat being offered on a silver tray. "How was Thanksgiving?"

"Just fine. We have a wonderful time with all the family together. I'd take it that Lady Elsmere was not too much of a burden," chatted Charles.

"I'm sitting right here, Charles," rebuked June. "I'm old, but I can hear fine."

"I know," Charles replied before leaving the room with a smile on his face. He loved to tease June.

"He thinks just because he's my heir that he can torment me."

"You mean by not kowtowing to your every whim? If you don't want Charles, I'll take him. I simply adore him."

June waved her hand in dismissal at me. "You couldn't afford him for a week, let alone full time. Let's get back to Ginny Wheelwright. Now that's juicy. What did you say when she told you to piss off?"

"Nothing. I'm not going to get into a catfight with a grieving mother. I picked up my cane and left, hoping that she'll come to her senses sooner or later."

"So you think Dwight Wheelwright died in a fishing accident and is lying at the bottom of the Cumberland Falls?"

"I didn't say that. I said that I thought Selena's grief was real."

"But you think that Dwight is dead?"

I shrugged my shoulders. "I don't know what to think. None of this makes any sense."

"What about the chocolate horse? Doesn't it seem strange that it had blood on it and that Selena threw it in the garbage on the day Dwight went missing?"

"That has bothered me as well as Dwight's cap being found in the water six weeks after he went missing and that it looked new."

"How do you know that it was Dwight's cap?"

"His name was written on the underside with a permanent marker."

"I think he ran off with another woman."

"You always think things have to do with sex."

"Well, don't they?" replied June, looking snide.

"I'm just going to ignore that. If your bones weren't so brittle, you'd still be bouncing on the sheets."

"You really need to get a checkup, Josiah. A woman your age is not ready to 'give it all up.' You're only fifty-one."

I chuckled. "The last thing I need is a man."

"You're not bad looking since your friend Irene cleaned you up and Franklin took over buying your clothes."

"If any man saw me naked, he'd go blind."

"That nice-looking Choctaw from Oklahoma seemed to be interested."

"And he ran home to his ex-wife the first chance he got."

June yawned, "At least you got some before he left town."

"Can we stay on point?"

"If you aren't going to give me any juicy details, then we need to hurry. I might fall asleep any moment from the sheer dullness of that thing you call your life."

"Well, now I've forgotten why I came to talk to you," I muttered.

It didn't matter, for Lady Elsmere was nodding off in her chair.

Sighing with frustration, I tiptoed to the library door.

"Love you," whispered the wizened old lady.

"Love you too, you old bat," I returned, looking affectionately at June.

She was fast asleep.

17

It was an unusually warm day in December. Since the temperature was hovering around sixty degrees, I checked on the bees.

Lighting my smoker, I quietly lifted the outer cover of the hive, smoking the hole of the inner cover before putting the lid down. After waiting a minute, I took the outer cover off and poured more smoke down the hole of the inner cover again.

Since there was no one to help me, I had to put down my smoker and take off the inner cover with my hive tool.

It didn't get any better than this. The bees were calm and regarded me with benign indifference.

With the hive tool, I scraped off some burr comb before pulling out a frame and inspecting it. The bees looked fat and happy clinging to the frame that held honey and pollen. There was no sign of disease . . . or the Queen for that matter. But Queens are rarely seen, as they like to hide.

Lowering my face close to the bees, I took a deep breath, trying to sniff out any bad odors, which signal something foul. Nothing amiss.

Before closing the hive, I put patties of bee pollen on top of the nine frames as a little added precaution in case the bees ran out of food during the winter. I'd rather be safe than sorry when it comes to my bees' health.

As a final inspection, I tried to move the hive with my knee. If it didn't move, the bees had plenty of honey. If the hive shifted, then the bees needed to be fed sugar water, as they would starve without it. (I refuse to use corn syrup.) Most beekeepers lose hives in late winter due to starvation more than any other cause. That's why I always put in extra pollen patties . . . just in case.

I had worked fifteen hives when I felt my cell phone vibrate. (Honeybees do not take kindly to noise.) Since I couldn't use it while wearing my bee suit, I jumped in my little golf cart and moved some distance away from the bee yard, and removed my veil.

"Hello? Hello? Darn it." I had missed the call. Struggling to remember how to get a voice message, I finally punched in the right code and listened to the message. Immediately, I returned the call.

"Selena?"

"Oh, Mrs. Reynolds! Thank goodness you returned my call. I didn't know who else to talk to."

"What's the problem?"

"Ginny was over here making all sorts of threats. She's totally off her rocker. I told her if she didn't stop with this nonsense about Dwight, I wasn't going to let her see the baby. I thought she was going to hit me. You should have seen Ginny's face.

"Mrs. Reynolds, can you talk to her? If she doesn't calm down, I'm going to have to issue a restraining order. I'm beginning to fear for my safety."

"Did you call the police?" I inquired.

"No, but I will if she comes back. I really will."

"Selena, lock your doors. Then sit down and have a nice cup of hot tea. That will do wonders to calm your nerves," I advise. "I can't talk to Ginny today. I'm working my bees, but I will see what I can do. But I'm not promising anything, you understand."

"I would be so grateful if you can do anything with her. I don't want to hurt Ginny, but she has got to stop or I am going to lose my mind!" Selena pleaded.

"I understand. I know her pastor. Maybe he can talk to her."

"That would be wonderful. Just any help at all would be great. I don't want to cause trouble with Ginny. I'm very fond of her and wouldn't like to see her get into trouble. Thanks so much, Mrs. Reynolds. I knew I could count on you."

The phone went silent. So Selena could count on me, eh. Well, I would see about that.

18

"I didn't threaten her. Not really threaten, I mean," justified Ginny, standing defiantly in the middle of her living room.

"You must have done something to make her mad."

"It's none of your beeswax."

"Very funny. Look, I'm trying to help you, Ginny, but I'm getting tired of you being a bitch. You asked me to help you and that's what I've been trying to do, but you are being as difficult as difficult can be. I'm done if you don't straighten up. I mean it," I threatened.

Ginny looked at me with undisguised hatred before exploding into tears. She looked like a fountain with all that water and her glass eye flipping in her eye socket for effect.

I had the sudden urge to laugh, but knew it would be in poor taste. Biting my lip, I tried to stifle the mirth I felt sliding up my esophagus threatening to escape my mouth. She just looked so pitiful.

As if to add to this comic scene, the glass eye kept flipping so fast that it popped out and hit me in the face.

Suddenly Ginny was gasping for breath and grabbing at her chest.

Now–that wasn't funny. I helped her into a chair.

"Ginny! Ginny! What's wrong? Are you having a heart attack?"

"Don't know. Jo, find my eye for me."

I looked about and spied it under a chair. With my cane, I fished it out and handed it to her.

Sucking the eye clean, Ginny then put it back in her eye socket. Blinking, she got the eye side to flip up.

"I'm going to call 911," I uttered, looking around for a phone.

Ginny grabbed my arm. "Don't. I feel better now. I don't think it was a heart attack. Just stress."

"I think a doctor should see you."

"I promise to go tomorrow. Just sit with me for a while, will ya, Jo?"

"I don't know," I replied wearily. "I really think you should see someone today."

"Get me a glass of water, hon, and I'll tell you why I'm so angry with Selena."

I hurried into the kitchen and brought back a glass of water for her. Pulling up a chair, I sat next to Ginny and felt her pulse. It seemed to be normal, as did her color, and she wasn't breathing hard.

After taking several sips, she handed the glass back to me. "I know I'm being a bother." She grabbed my hand. "Jo, you gotta believe me. A mother knows. Something is very wrong and it starts in my son's house. I know it has something to do with Selena. I bet my life on it."

I shook my head. "I don't agree, Ginny. I'm sorry, but there it is."

Ginny pulled away and was lost in thought.

I was tired of all the drama, but I didn't want to leave her in this state. I was racking my brains for someone to call to take over. I had done my part.

"Jo? Let's say you're right that Selena had nothing to do with Dwight's disappearance."

"I'm listening."

"Would you look at the police file and tell me what you think?"

"You should really talk to the detectives working the case, or hire a private investigator."

"Their minds don't work like yours."

"How's that?"

"They follow rules. You ain't got no rules."

19

"You really gotta refine that interrogation technique of yours," laughed Detective Goetz. "This makes how many people who have needed medical attention after talking with you? First there was your husband, who after a fight with you, has a heart attack and dies."

"That's a low blow. His death wasn't my fault," I protested.

"Then there was a guy named Ison Taggert who didn't even wait until you left, but has a heart attack in front of you," Goetz countered.

"He had a panic attack. How do you know about him anyway?"

"I have connections with the Richmond police. He needed to go to the hospital . . . right? Now your friend,

Ginny Wheelwright. Remind me not to get into a heated discussion with you."

"Her doctor said it was due to stress and high blood pressure. Ginny's a ticking time bomb unless she slows down."

"Again, while talking with you. That's the point. You're a walking dip stick of misery."

"A dip stick of misery. Let me write that down. That's sheer poetry. Are you going to look into Dwight Wheelwright's disappearance or not?" I demanded.

"No. We did our part. It's up to the boys at the State Police and Whitley County to do theirs. But I can tell you that they did their job. There is nothing more to do until a body is found or Dwight Wheelwright pops up alive somewhere."

"Let's say he was murdered for a reason and not due to a botched robbery. Whom would you suspect?"

"His mother. She had the motive of the life insurance policy."

"That's ridiculous. Ginny couldn't harm a fly, let alone her own flesh and blood," I hissed.

"You'd be surprised what people will do for money, regardless of blood ties."

"What about his wife, Selena?"

"No motive. His daughter gets the money, which is held in trust until she is eighteen. But I really don't think his relatives killed him. You know that. He was killed by a stranger in Whitley County and is buried in the forest. He may have stumbled upon a marijuana patch in the woods and was killed over that . . . or a robbery that went down bad. He was driving a sweet pickup. Maybe someone wanted his ride, then got scared and ran off."

"And you think that because Dwight's hat was found weeks after his disappearance?"

"Why the rehash? I've told you all this before. You must be fishing for something. Let's change the subject. I shouldn't be talking with you about the case anyway." Goetz eyed the cake carrier I was holding in my lap. "Is that my lemon pound cake?"

"Yes," I replied in a deflated voice as I handed the cake carrier to him.

"Explain to Ginny Wheelwright that everything that could be done has been done. Until we get a break, it remains a cold case."

I got up to leave. "Goetz. You don't think I was really responsible for my husband's death, do you?"

Goetz lifted his weary hound-dog face.

I had never noticed before what an intense blue his eyes were.

"I think you were so in love with your husband that you didn't recognize him for the jerk that he was. He got himself into a jam with a younger woman and couldn't find a way out, so he just took himself out of the game. That's all there was to it."

"You sound like you knew him."

"As a matter of fact, Josiah, I did know him." Goetz was quiet for a moment, and then he added, "I didn't like him."

20

After the meeting with Goetz, I still had enough energy to pick up a few things from the grocery store.

Maybe it was fate, kismet or whatever you want to call it, but I ran into the lab technician who had run the tests on Dwight's chocolate centerpiece.

"Oh, hi. Do you remember me? I did the tests on the chocolate horse centerpiece." She blocked my path to the fresh produce.

"Yes. Funny running into you. Do you live near here?" I'm always suspicious when I just bump into people.

She gave me a big smile. "I live in the apartments across the street. It's Mrs. Reynolds, right?"

"Yes. I'm sorry, but I don't remember your name."

"It's Charlotte. I'm glad I ran into you. I was going to give you a call."

"My check didn't bounce, did it?"

Charlotte gave a short laugh that sounded like water tinkling over some rocks.

"I forgot to give you something along with the report."

"What is it?" I asked, intrigued.

"I found human hair on the chocolate caked in the blood. I put the hairs in a vial and meant to put it in the return container, but it was a busy day and I forgot. So I was going to mail it to you. I'm very sorry for the mix-up. I hope you don't report me to my boss."

"No, I won't report you. Do you remember if the hair was from the same person or different people?"

Charlotte put her finger to her mouth, remembering. "There were only four hairs, short, brown."

"Did you do a DNA profile on them?"

"No, that wasn't asked for. There was nothing on the application that requested hair sampling."

"Can you do a DNA profile on them?"

"Of course," Charlotte responded cheerfully.

"Can you compare DNA from another strand of hair if provided?"

"Certainly."

"Do me a favor, will you, Charlotte?" I asked.

"If it's not illegal," she answered, grinning.

"Keep the hair. I'm going to find another sample and have a complete DNA analysis done."

"Super." Charlotte gave a quizzical look.

"This could be the answer to the disappearance of a friend of mine."

"Cool. Just like CSI. Just ask for me to do the sampling. It's Charlotte. Can you remember that?"

I repeated her name. "Yes. Thank you, Charlotte."

"Bye."

I hurried to my car, but by the time I found a piece of paper, I had forgotten her name.

Jumping Jehosaphat!

21

After racking my brain trying to remember the technician's name, I remembered that I had not gotten any groceries. So into the store I marched again with a list that Eunice had written for me. She was cooking for me once a week and storing the dinners in the walk-in freezer. So all I had to do was nuke them.

This was on top of her duties besides planning and executing the tours and receptions now held at the Butterfly.

I don't really see how she did it all.

But her cooking saved me from a lot of stress as I couldn't stand very long, and it was too frustrating to cook. With my short-term memory loss, I couldn't recall recipes anymore.

After my fall, nothing with my body was the same as before. One never appreciates good health until it fails. Well, let's not dwell on that. It's too depressing.

Putting the groceries in the front passenger's seat (so I wouldn't forget them), I looked up and noticed a dark blue sedan with tinted windows parked not too far from me. It looked like the same blue sedan that I had seen on other occasions.

Was someone following me?

Were there two cars that looked alike?

Was it coincidence?

Was I losing my mind?

It was time I found out for sure.

Gathering a pad and pencil, which I slid into my coat pocket, I walked my grocery cart, presumably over to its collection bin. Somehow the cart slipped out of my hands and rolled toward the blue sedan, hitting it square on its bumper. It made a little dent. (Funny how that happened as the cart had to roll uphill. Maybe it had been pushed a little bit.)

No one jumped out of the car in outrage to inspect the damage. Assured that no one was in the car, I retrieved the cart and sidled my way to the back of the sedan where I quickly wrote down the license plate number.

I've killed two birds with one stone, I thought to myself.

What a lucky day at the grocery store!

22

Once I had gotten home and helped Eunice put away the groceries, I sat down at my office desk and began to make a list of people in Dwight's life, starting with those closest to him.

Ginny/Mother – Had the motive of the insurance money, but I just wrote her off as a suspect. It was too creepy to think she had something to do with her son's death.

Daughter – Too young.

Selena/Wife – Maybe, but I didn't think so. No discernable motive.

Farley Webb/Partner – Maybe, but no discernable motive.

Business Clients – No motive.

Unknown – Unforeseeable, like a robbery.
Psycho – Statistics were against it.

Maybe Goetz was right. Maybe Dwight was buried in some shallow grave because he stumbled across a marijuana patch or because someone wanted his truck.

Still, we had to rule out the obvious first. Although I didn't think Selena and Farley had anything to do with Dwight's disappearance, I needed to prove it. They had to be ruled out first, before the hunt for Dwight's killer . . . if there was one . . . continued in another direction.

I scratched my head and then licked the pencil lead. A nervous habit since my accident. I began to write a long list of questions that needed to be answered. After finishing three legal pages of questions, I looked at the clock and saw it was after midnight.

"Oh, dear," I said. "I'm late." Quickly I went to my bedroom.

There stood Baby waiting at the glass door that led to the patio. He gave me an irritated look.

"I know. I know. Time just got away from me."
I opened the door to let in Baby's pet cats, which spent the day in the barn and came to the house every night to sleep with Baby. They had been born in my closet. Last, but not least, straggled in Mama Cat, who would not even lower herself to cast a glance in my direction.

"You're welcome," I chided.

The next half hour was spent keeping cats out of my bed, away from my toothbrush and hand soap, off the window drapes and my vanity.

"Come on, guys. Settle down," I begged. "I have to get up early and see Ginny."

Didn't these animals understand that? Apparently not, as they kept me up for another hour.

I hope Baby was satisfied.

23

"You got any of Dwight's hair?"

"I have some locks from when he was a child. Why?"

"Give me some."

"How much?"

"Can you give me an entire lock? That should be enough."

Ginny seemed undecided. It was hard to give away your baby's hair when that was all you had left of the baby.

"It seems that we didn't ask enough from the testing lab. They found some hair on the chocolate and it's human. I think we should compare it to Dwight's. You in or out?"

Ginny gave me a smile that would light up the darkest cave. "That's the Jo I know. I'm in. What next?"

"Give me a check." I told her how much it would cost.

Her smile fell. "I'll have to take out a loan. Can it wait a few days until I get things settled?"

"Sure. There's no hurry. You can still back out." I gave Ginny a moment. "Are you sure you really want to pursue this?"

"I don't trust the cops to look for my boy anymore, Jo. They have other cases and they think Dwight ran off. I've got to see this through."

I didn't relate that Detective Goetz thought he was dead and buried under a pile of leaves in the Daniel Boone National Forest. Some things one should keep to oneself. "Okay. I understand. Ginny, is there any reason Dwight would always go to the Cumberland area to fish? Why not Herrington Lake, which is closer?"

"My people are from that area. Dwight usually goes to the old homestead and checks on the family cemetery. I used to take him there as a child."

"Oh, I wasn't aware of that. Do you still have kin there?"

"Everyone's gone now, but Dwight's familiar with the area and has happy memories. You know my family was originally from Tennessee but moved up to the Cumberland. I'm a relative of Julia Marcum, being a direct descendant of her daddy. Marcum's my maiden name."

"I didn't know that. I've heard of her, but don't really know her story."

"As I said, my family lived in Tennessee, but were Union sympathizers. We didn't hold with slavery.

"When Julia was sixteen, Confederate soldiers came looking for her daddy. After interrogating Julia, they left . . . all but one soldier. A life and death struggle broke out between Julia and the soldier.

"Perhaps the soldier was trying to make Julia talk or maybe he was going to rape her. Who knows why the fight started, but he stabbed Julia in the eye with his bayonet.

"Wounded, she struck him with an ax. Still alive, the soldier managed to shoot one of her fingers off.

"It was then her father rushed in and killed the soldier. The family fled to Kentucky, where Julia lived out her life and died in Whitley County at the age of ninety-one in 1936. She was one of the few women who received a pension from the United States for having fought in the Civil War."

I pointed to Ginny's glass eye. "Sight issues for the women folk seem to run in your family."

Ginny's hand glanced over her bad eye. "I never connected the two since I lost my eye in a boating accident, but you're right. It's the same eye."

"Interesting."

"Anything else?"

"I think it's time to visit Cumberland Falls."

24

The Cumberland River was called Wasioto by Native Americans and Riviere Des Chaouanons (River of the Shawnee) by French traders.

In 1750, it was renamed by Dr. Thomas Walker for Prince William, Duke of Cumberland.

The Cumberland River is six hundred eighty-eight miles long, beginning in eastern Kentucky, dipping into Tennessee to Nashville and then snaking back through Kentucky to merge with the Ohio River near Paducah, just a few miles away from the great Mississippi River.

Its great claim to fame is the Cumberland Falls, which has the only Moonbeam Rainbow in the western hemisphere.

Cumberland Falls straddles both Whitley and McCreary Counties with a 125-foot curtain and falls 68 feet with the average flow of 3,600 cubic feet per second.

Much of the park is in Whitley County, which is named after William Whitley, a renowned frontiersman and Indian fighter, though he never lived in Whitley County. He is considered a war hero from the Battle of the Thames, a decisive battle of the War of 1812.

He built the first brick house in Kentucky and altered how horse racing was (and still is) run in America. He built a racecourse that had the horses run counter-clockwise, which was a snub at how the English raced theirs . . . clockwise.

He first came to Kentucky in 1775. He and his family journeyed through the Cumberland Gap to the current town of Stanford, where Whitley planted ten acres of corn to stake his land claim.

That being done, Whitley moved his family to the safety of Fort Harrod in Harrodsburg, Kentucky. It was during this time that Whitley beheld a horrible sight, which twisted his mind for the remainder of his life.

Whitley saw the body of William Ray, who had been mutilated by Native Americans, most probably the Shawnee. It was the first time that he had seen a man scalped.

Unlike frontiersmen Daniel Boone and Simon Kenton, who respected the Indians, Whitley thought they were savages and spent a great deal of his life fighting them and removing their scalps as trophies.

He became so enamored of this bizarre custom that he requested of General William Henry Harrison that if Whitley should die under his command, Harrison was to return his scalp to his wife, Esther, along with his horse, Emperor.

Whitley led the charge against Tecumseh and was reported by many eyewitnesses to be the man who actually slew the great Shawnee chief rather than Richard Johnson, later the ninth Vice President of the United States, who took the credit.

It is not known who struck down Whitley during the battle. He was sixty-four years old.

Emperor had lost one eye and two teeth during the battle's charge and was returned to Whitley's family, along with Whitley's powder horn, strap, and rifle.

Most folks know little about the Battle of the Thames, which took place near Chatham, Ontario on October 5, 1813.

Simon Kenton claimed that he was asked to identify Tecumseh's body but lied, as he didn't want the great chief's body to be mutilated by the whites. As he leaned over the body of Tecumseh, he muttered, "There be cowards here." He pointed to another Native American's body as that of the Shawnee chief.

Of the 3,500 infantry and cavalry commanded by Harrison, five brigades were Kentuckians led by Isaac Shelby, Kentucky's first governor, as well as 1,000 Kentucky volunteer cavalry under Richard Johnson from Georgetown, Kentucky.

But Ginny and I weren't concerned with the history of the Cumberland River as we stared at the tumultuous pool below the river's most fantastic site—the thundering Cumberland Falls.

Ginny's face twisted in grief as she grabbed my arm. "You don't think my boy's down there in that mess, do you?"

I looked down sixty-eight feet to the turbulent pool where the Falls collided with the river again. "No, Ginny, they've already dragged the pool. He's not there."

"Yes, that's right. I would hate to think of Dwight under all that water."

"Are you going to be all right with this? I can come back by myself." I knew I had made a mistake bringing her. Ginny was just too tender yet.

"I won't get in the way, promise. In fact, I'll go sit in the Lodge until you're finished, Jo."

"I think that would be best. People might be hesitant to speak in front of you . . . being the mother and all."

"I understand. I won't be difficult, I promise. I've got my cell phone. Call if you need me."

Leaving Ginny to rest at Dupont Lodge, I headed out of the park onto US 25 and then on the Bee Creek Road for the Grove Marina on Laurel River Lake.

Laurel River Lake is a reservoir built in 1977 by the U.S. Army Corps of Engineers on the Laurel River.

Once in the Daniel Boone National Forest, I opened the car windows.

The temperature was definitely cooler outside and the

air seemed dank and musty. I drove slowly, taking in the dense, deep green forest on both sides of the road.

Goetz was right. Someone could be buried in the forest and no one would find the body for years, if at all. I shook that notion out of my head. One had to be positive. Goodness, what was I thinking? I didn't want Dwight's body to be found at all. I wanted him to be alive and trying to get back to his family.

Still, Ginny needed to know for sure.

I pulled into the nicely landscaped Marina's parking lot and parked in the handicapped section. Using my ebony cane, which Franklin had purchased for me in Key West, I managed my way down the long plank to the General Store. I stepped up my pace when two fishermen in wheelchairs, dragging a huge ice chest, whizzed past me and onto a fishing boat.

After having yelled at me good-naturedly to get out of the way when passing, they then beckoned to me to come join them on the boat. I don't think they had fishing in mind.

Grinning, I waved goodbye and hurried into the General Store. At the front counter, I asked for Billy Klotter, the person who had found Dwight's rented boat adrift on the lake.

"Billy!" yelled a disheveled bosomy woman at the front counter. "Someone here to see you." She then motioned for me to stand out of the way so she could wait on customers.

A man about my age, with salt and pepper hair, shuffled out of the back room. He must have had arthritis, as his movements were stiff and slow. "Yep?" he said, looking around the store.

I waved to him and stepped behind the counter. The bosomy woman gave me an irritated look and was about to say something when I rushed some words out. "Mr. Klotter, I am Josiah Reynolds. I called earlier about Dwight Wheelwright. Can we step into your office? Great. Thank you," I proposed as I stepped around Mr. Klotter and marched into his sanctuary.

There was no way I was going to discuss this around a bunch of nosey locals who were straining their necks to get a look at me.

Mr. Klotter had no choice but to follow.

I took possession of a ratty duct-taped recliner and waited for Mr. Klotter to ease himself into a chair behind his desk cluttered with fishing paraphernalia and paperwork.

Opening a folder, I took out a picture of Dwight and handed it to Mr. Klotter. "Mr. Klotter, is this the man you rented a boat to on July third of this year?"

Mr. Klotter took the photo in hand and fished out a battered folder on his desk. He compared the picture to something in the folder. "To the best of my recollection, yes. This is the same man."

"May I ask what you are looking at?"

Billy Klotter handed back the photo and a stained 8x10 sheet of paper. On it was a photocopy of Dwight's driver's license.

"According to our records, the man in this photograph rented that boat."

"May I have a copy please?"

"No problem. Yep."

"But can you identify just from the photograph that I handed you that this was the same man who rented the boat and then went missing on the third?"

Billy Klotter shook his head. "No, ma'am. No one who worked on that day can do that. When we rent out a boat, we ask for a credit card deposit and make a copy of their driving and fishing license. That's for our protection. As you can see, here is his credit card slip. I'll make a copy of that for you too. Maybe you can have his handwriting analyzed, but as far as we are concerned that man in your photo rented a fishing boat on July third. We would never claim to identify him from a photo. We can't, due to the sheer number of people we serve. After awhile, everyone looks the same. You see?"

I was disappointed. I was hoping that Mr. Klotter would point to the photograph and state, "Why–that is not the man who rented the boat!"

"Can you tell me what happened on the third?"

Klotter peered at his paperwork. "Mr. Wheelwright rented the boat around 9 a.m. and should have been back at 6 p.m. Around 7 p.m. I went out looking for him. It's not unusual for people to become lost or run out of gas.

"I found the boat forty minutes later. It was empty, but contained his wallet. It was lying on the floor of the boat. The gas tank was almost full. I called the local authorities, who called the state cops." Mr. Klotter shrugged. "And that was that."

"Wait a minute," I said, looking at my notes. "You said his wallet was in the boat. The police report says that his wallet was found in his pickup's glove compartment."

Billy shook his head again. "I found the man's wallet on the floor of that boat in a puddle of dirty water. That's how I confirmed whose boat it was."

"What happened to the wallet?"

"I gave it to the local boys."

"Do they still have it?"

"Couldn't say," Billy sputtered.

I made a note to check about the wallet.

"And was the lake dragged?"

"Parts of it. Even scuba divers went down. They didn't find nothing."

"Just parts? Why not the entire lake? After all, a man was missing."

"The entire shoreline was searched but lady, this lake is nineteen miles in length with an average depth of sixty-five feet with the maximum depth being two hundred and eighty feet. The total shore length itself is two hundred and six miles long. We did all we could, considering."

"I see. What happens when someone drowns and you can't find them?"

"Don't mean to be indelicate, but they usually pop up sooner or later."

"Billy, need your help out here!" yelled the bosomy woman.

"Coming," rejoined Billy, rising from his desk. "Ma'am, we're awful busy."

"Just a few more questions, please. You seem like an observant man. What did you observe?"

Mr. Klotter thought for a moment.

"Billy!!!!"

"Hold your horses, woman! Coming." Mr. Klotter turned toward me.

"I thought it odd that the man's wallet was lying loose in the boat. Most fishermen are afraid of losing their wallets, so they put them up in one of the containers or storage areas provided on the boat.

"And his fishin' pole was gone. I found it tangled in some weeds later. That was to be expected if he had fallen into the water, but the funny thing was, there were no fish on the boat. Nary a one. He must have fallen in very early in the morning before he caught anything."

"Was there any sign of violence or blood? Was the boat damaged in any way?" I inquired.

"You should ask one of the State boys on that, but I didn't see anything. No, nothing comes to mind."

"BILLY!!!!!!!"

Mr. Klotter shot a sympathetic look at me.

"Just one more question, please. How long does it take for a body to surface?"

"Usually a couple of weeks, but it has been known to happen a month or two later, but then it's just parts. The fish get to them. You know what I mean. Sorry to be so graphic, but it is what it is and you seem like a plain-speaking woman."

I nodded in concurrence. "And nothing has been found of the man in your folder?" I stated, pointing to Mr. Klotter's file.

"Not that I'm aware of. It would seem that if he was in the lake, something would have been found of him by now."

"Mr. Klotter, do you think Mr. Wheelwright is in Laurel Lake?"

"BILLY!!!!!!!!!!!!!!!!"

Mr. Klotter gave a steely look. "No, ma'am. I do not!"

And with that pronouncement, Mr. Klotter showed me the door.

25

Before joining Ginny, I went to the front desk at Dupont Lodge.

"Hello," I said to one of the ugliest men I had ever seen. He was wearing thick glasses that made his eyes look huge and had faint gray stubble on his cheeks, giving his skin an unhealthy pallor. The effect reminded me of a used brillo pad.

A story about Abraham Lincoln's less than handsome appearance immediately came to mind. Abe ran across a woman who exclaimed, "I do believe you are the ugliest man I ever saw!" To which Abe replied, "Madam, you are probably right, but I can't help it." Without hesitation, she rejoined, "No, you can't help it, but you might stay at home."

Trying not to chuckle at my own insipid thoughts, I asked, "I was wondering if you could help me?"

"I'll certainly try," he answered cheerfully, giving me his full attention.

I looked at his badge, on which was printed the name Steve. Steve might be so ugly that he frightened babies, but I could tell that he tried to be a good man. You could just tell from his demeanor.

"How long have you worked here?"

He scratched his face as if considering this an odd question. Deciding that there was no harm in answering, he replied, "About seven months now."

I pulled out the picture of Dwight. "I am investigating the disappearance of Dwight Wheelwright." I held up the picture of Dwight. "I was wondering if you had ever seen this man?"

He took a hard look at the picture. "That's the man that went missing some time back. I thought the police had decided that he had just up and run away."

"His family doesn't think so." I shook the picture a little.

"Are you the police?" the young man asked, pronouncing police as Pole-leeese, "'cause I've already answered these questions several times."

"I'm authorized by the man's mother to investigate."

"Oh, his mama. I see. Well then, I'll tell you what I told the police. I can identify that man as Dwight Wheelwright, who checked in here on July first. He said he was going fishing up Bee Creek Road. Was gonna check out on the third, because he had a birthday party to go to. Said it was his."

I looked at my map of the area. "I don't see where Bee Creek Road hits the lake."

Steve leaned over the counter and traced a route with a pen. "You have to go on Bee Creek Road first, then turn here to go to Grove Marina. That takes you deep into Daniel Boone National Forest and then to the lake."

"Oh, I see," I said, deflated. "I just came from Grove Marina. I now remember I had to turn off US 25. That must have been Bee Creek Road. Thank you." I didn't want to bore the young man with how I forgot little things like names of roads now. I started to walk away and then got a flash of inspiration.

Maybe my brain wasn't that dull after all. "You said this is what you told the police. Was there something you didn't tell the police?"

Steve looked about to see if anyone was listening.

There was not another person in sight.

Steve leaned over the counter in a conspiratorial manner. "He made a big deal about this party. Was real chatty. Most people just want their room key and credit card back in a hurry. He hung around."

I now knew Steve was a fountain of information, but one had to ask the right questions.

"Steve . . . may I call you Steve . . . what kind of an accent did he have? Did he have one like yours?"

"No, ma'am. He wasn't from these parts. He had a city accent like from up north or around the Cincinnati area. Sorta like yours."

"Was it more midwestern than mine, you think?"

"Could be, but it wasn't an accent from upper Midwest like Michigan or the Dakotas. I meet people from all around the world. You get to recognize the accents, you know."

I thought that very interesting, as Dwight had a thick Kentucky accent, which he could never shake. "Take a look at this picture again. Are you a hundred percent sure that this is the man that checked in?"

Steve pushed his glasses further up on his nose. "Yeah, that's the man. Of course, it's hard to tell 'cause he's not wearing a hat in the picture."

"Dwight was wearing a hat when he checked in?"

"A fishing hat, but he had it pulled down low."

"Was it a hat with a bass embroidered on it?"

"I guess. I don't really remember what was on it except that it had a long bill."

"Tell me, if the hat was pulled low, could you see his eyes?"

"Well, rightly no, but I know this is the same man. I'd swear on the Bible. Of course, Darlene doesn't think so."

"And who'd be Darlene?"

"Usually Darlene works the night shift, but she was working the morning shift that day when Mr.

Wheelwright checked out. She told the police that the man who checked out wasn't the man in the picture they'd showed her, but I set them right after they talked to me."

"I see. Is Darlene still working here?" I asked, barely able to contain my excitement.

"She's in the dining room getting something to eat before she comes on shift."

"Thank you, Steve. You've been a big help."

Steve beamed. "Always glad to be of assistance."

I hurried to the dining room. The elevator could not go fast enough. Finally reaching the dining room, I stepped into an expansive wood-beamed room originally built by the CCC boys (Civilian Conservation Corps) in 1933 and then rebuilt in 1941 after a fire. The entire back wall was glass with bird feeding stations along a majestic view of the Cumberland River.

Next to one of the picture windows sat a middle-aged blond watching the birds while sipping coffee. She had on a name tag.

I approached her table trying to read her tag. "Darlene?"

"Yes," she replied, looking up cautiously.

I could tell that she didn't want to be disturbed. This was probably her quiet time before going on her shift. "My name is Josiah Reynolds. I'm sorry to bother you, but I have a few questions to ask you about the Dwight Wheelwright case. I understand that you checked him out?"

"Who are you?"

"I'm authorized by Mr. Wheelwright's mother to investigate his disappearance. Can you help me please? Steve said that you didn't think the man that you checked out was this man?" I held out Dwight's photo.

Darlene gave a big sigh. "Steve's got a big mouth. Nice man, but no sense. You know the type. So that fellow never got found, huh?

"I'll tell you what I told the police. The picture they showed me was not the same man who checked out. Let me see yours." Darlene took the picture out of my hand and studied it carefully. "It's hard to tell from this picture to make a positive ID, but if he's got a tiny white scar on his chin, then that's not him."

She peered closer at the picture, moving her coffee cup out of the way. "I don't see a scar on this picture. This is not the man that I checked out on July third. I'd swear on my mama's Bible."

JACKPOT! Dwight didn't have any scars on his face.

Darlene tapped the picture with her glossy pink fingernail. "Whoever this is, I hoped he took my advice and went to the hospital."

"Why is that?"

"He was in awful pain from a scorpion bite. Limping so hard he could barely make it to his car. Felt sorry for him. Those bites are dangerous if not taken care of."

"Scorpions?"

"The Devil Scorpion. People need to be careful in this area. We've got scads of them."

"How do you know that it was a scorpion that was causing his limp?"

"He told me so. Said he got stung by a scorpion. There is no way that man got into a boat and went fishing all day. He needed pain medication and a doctor."

I shuddered. I knew I had Brown Recluse and Black Widow spiders on the farm, but scorpions? Yuck!

"Anything else that stands out to you?"

"Naw. Hope you find your man, though." Darlene handed the picture back and resumed her coffee drinking, looking out the windows at the birds feeding.

I had been dismissed.

26

I told Ginny what I had learned.

"Oh, dear. This just gets worse and worse."

"What do you mean?"

"Dwight didn't like to fish on boats. He was not a good swimmer and Laurel Lake being so deep and all . . . he liked to go fly-fishing or fish from the bank. It wasn't his nature to rent a boat. Dwight was frightened of the lake."

"Don't you have to wade in the water for fly fishing?" I asked.

"Depends on the type of fly fishing, but there is a difference between wading into a river that only comes up to your knees and fishing from an unsteady boat on a deep lake. See the difference if you might be shy around deep water? That's why he preferred the Cumberland River. I was always suspicious of this boat thing. I thought it out of character."

"I see."

Ginny continued. "Of course, the best place to go fly fishing for trout is below Wolf Creek Dam at Cumberland Lake. That's where Dwight would go fly fishing."

I shook my head. "I'm confused."

"You see, Jo, fishing is an art form. You fish differently for each type of fish you want."

"Did Dwight tell you what type of fish he wanted to catch?"

"Don't recall."

"Ginny, were you anxious about Dwight's swimming ability?"

"Oh, yes, very. He wasn't a good swimmer at all."

It now occurred to me that perhaps Dwight lied to his mother about lake fishing because he didn't want to alarm her that he was in a boat. Lying would save him grief, and Ginny concern. Maybe he did rent a boat and fell into the lake, drowning, and now his body was snagged by some underwater tree.

Still, there was Darlene saying the man that checked out as Dwight had a scar on his chin, which the real Dwight did not. And if he had been stung by a scorpion, would he really rent a boat instead of seeing a doctor?

What to do? What to do?

27

"Darlene said that Dwight was not the man she checked out. You need to reopen this case."

Goetz shifted his weight in his chair. "Darlene who?"

"I didn't get her last name, but she works at Dupont Lodge and she said Dwight was not the man she checked on July third. Now she says the man she checked out was limping from a scorpion bite . . ."

"A what?" interrupted Goetz.

"A scorpion bite and he was limping. If Dwight were stung by a scorpion, he would have gone to a doctor. He wouldn't have gone fishing."

"Men are notorious for not going to a doctor when they need to, especially if it would interfere with something they want to do. And they don't like to complain that they are in pain. I can see a man trying to go fishing until he was in so much pain he couldn't stand it, or he fell out of the boat because he got dizzy from the pain."

"Farley Webb never showed up at Dwight's birthday party."

"So?"

"There's more. Darlene said the man she checked out had a tiny white scar on his chin. Farley Webb has a tiny white scar on his chin."

"Did you have her ID a picture of Farley Webb?"

"No, but I showed her a picture of Dwight and she said that was not the man she checked out. She's positive."

"Did you ever see Farley Webb limp? Or did he tell you he got bitten by a scorpion?"

"Well, no. Like I said, he didn't come to the party, so I never saw him."

"Has anyone else ever said they saw Farley Webb limping . . . like the guy at the Grove Marina who rented out the boat?"

My voice was barely audible. "No, but there was no reason until now to ask those questions. I didn't know to ask Mr. Klotter that question."

"Don't you think he would have mentioned it? Did Ginny say she saw Farley Webb limping?"

"No, but . . ."

"But . . . but . . . but. Awful lot of buts."

Fuming, I huffed, "He was supposed to be Dwight's best friend and he doesn't show up for Dwight's birthday party? Come on, now. You need to check emergency hospital records for someone with a scorpion bite."

"You know how many hospitals and clinics are between Cumberland Falls and here? Besides, I hate to tell you this, but most men don't really care for girlie birthday parties. We'd rather have a nice steak dinner with our wives and then go home and have birthday sex. I can see why Mr. Webb wanted to skip his friend's party."

"It's your job to look into this, isn't it?"

"What's this Darlene's last name?" Goetz asked again.

"I told you that I don't know. I didn't ask, but she works at the front desk at Dupont Lodge."

"Some detective you are . . . not asking for a last name. And I suppose you didn't get an address or phone number either?" quizzed Goetz, squinting his eyes at me.

"People won't talk to you if you start asking all these intrusive questions. That's where the law comes into play."

"I'm not convinced. You have to give me something more."

"What if Selena was having an affair with Farley Webb and they plotted Dwight's death because they thought Selena was the beneficiary of Dwight's insurance policy?"

"There is not one single shred of evidence to point to that conclusion."

"I've got a huge piece of chocolate with Dwight's blood and hair on it," I lied. (I hadn't gotten the report back yet.) "I think they hit him over the head killing him with the birthday chocolate. Then took the body to the Daniel Boone National Forest where they buried him."

"Do you know how stupid that sounds? A piece of chocolate? How can you kill someone by hitting them with candy?"

"You haven't seen this chocolate horse. It weighs twenty-three pounds."

"Selena didn't leave town during those three days and no one made any kind of statement that she seemed nervous or tense . . . like she had just murdered her husband. They said she seemed content and happy."

"Yeah. She thought she was coming into five hundred thousand big ones."

Goetz was quiet and stared out the window onto Main Street. The holiday lights twinkled on the Ginkgo trees as rush hour traffic buzzed by. It was drizzling. Heavy snow was predicted for later that night.

"Make me a Derby pie and I might consider it," Goetz demanded.

"Deal. I thought you were still going to lose more weight."

"My lady friend moved to Florida, so now I don't give a damn."

"I didn't know you had a lady friend."

Goetz remained quiet and began playing with a rubber band. He seemed to be aiming the rubber band at me.

He let go of it so that it whizzed past my ear, hitting the wall behind me.

That was my cue to leave.

I got out of there fast.

28

I had only seen Farley Webb several times and then had never really paid much attention to him. He was the type of man who bores me. Good-looking and knows it, with a head full of narcissism and ambition. He wasn't even that charming. I never knew what a down-home boy like Dwight saw in him.

Of course, one doesn't have to like one's business partner in order to do business. Maybe Farley put up the money for their venture.

"Hello, Mrs. Reynolds. Nice to see you again," crooned Farley as he swept me into his plush office. "Please have a seat." He looked at his secretary who stood beside me. "Would you like something to drink—coffee, tea, water? We've got it all."

"No thank you." I replied, admiring his tailored gray suit. *Armani,* I wondered.

Farley gave a curt nod to the woman who briskly left the room. "To what do I owe this pleasure?"

Could he get any smarmier?

"I'm sorry to bother you, Farley. I can see that you are very busy . . . and very successful. I must say I had no idea."

Farley smiled, showing his professionally whitened teeth, while playing with his silk tie. "I can't deny it. Dwight and I struck gold. We both worked our tails off, but it paid off as you can see." He was referring to the expensive mahogany office furniture and the several Henry Faulkner paintings on the wall. In a corner was a John Tuska sculpture.

"May I ask what is going to happen now that Dwight is gone?"

"I have control over the company and we will go on as before. Some of our clients don't even know that he is gone. Things have gone that smoothly."

Surprised at this, I reared back in my seat. "Really?"

"We both put clauses in our contract that if one of us was incapacitated for any reason, then the other partner would take over the reins. We thought this was fair to the other partner."

"What happens to the incapacitated partner's family?"

"The business buys them out."

I was quiet for a moment.

Farley looked concerned. "Don't worry, Mrs. Reynolds. Selena will receive excellent compensation and she doesn't want a thing to do with the company anyway."

"So it's win-win for everyone."

"Except for Dwight. May I be blunt, Mrs. Reynolds?"

"Of course."

"Why are you here? I've heard that you have been asking questions about Dwight's disappearance." Farley gave me another wide, bright smile. "You don't think I had anything to do with it, do you?"

I gave a small laugh. "Did you?"

Farley chuckled.

"Ginny asked me to look into Dwight's disappearance–not in an official capacity, but to help her resolve some issues. She is awfully confused at the moment and is giving Selena some reasons for concern. I'm just trying to help Ginny resolve some of her questions, so she can move on. To tell you the truth, I am concerned about Ginny. I hope you don't mind me being here asking some things."

Farley sighed . . . I think with relief. "If you put it that way, of course not. I want to help anyway I can. I know Ginny is having a terrible time and that she and Selena are butting heads. If you can resolve this conflict by asking some questions, go right ahead."

"Thank you. Did you and Dwight get along?"

"We were like brothers. Going into business with each other was the best thing we ever did."

"And the business is doing well?"

"Let me put it this way. I switch out my Mercedes every year."

"You're not married, are you?"

"Guilty as charged."

"Girlfriend?"

Farley gave me that cheesy grin again. "Lots of them."

"Everyone get along . . . you with Selena, the girlfriends?"

"Oh, I see. You want to know if there was woman trouble." Farley looked out the window. "No."

When someone doesn't look me in the eye when answering a direct question, a little bell never fails to go off in my head.

"Farley? Is that the honest truth? Whatever it is, it will be found out sooner or later."

He patted down his tie and then played with the pens on his desk as if trying to make up his mind about something.

I remained quiet, waiting for the man to speak.

Clearing his throat, Farley came out with, "I was trying to spare Ginny's feelings, but I know that Dwight is alive."

I nearly jumped out of my chair. "What!"

Farley took out his handkerchief and wiped his forehead. "We hired a new girl about a year ago. Well, Dwight went crazy over her and they started having an affair. He told me that he was really happy for the first time in his life, but he didn't want to hurt Selena or leave the baby. Dwight was in a quandary and didn't know what to do. I think he was hoping that the affair would blow over and he could go back to his normal life."

"Dwight never seemed like the cheating type."

"It took me by surprise, that is for sure. She left for a position out west a week before Dwight disappeared. I think he staged this disappearance so he could join her and start a new life."

"Why not divorce Selena first?"

"Who knows why people do the things they do. I think he was loco in love." Farley leaned forward. "We also are missing money from the accounts as well."

"How much?"

"Over two hundred thousand."

"Did you tell Selena this?"

"Why do you think she wants to move on with her life? If Dwight wants to be free of her, then she is going to cut him dead. She wants closure. Understand?"

"Why the memorial?"

"I think it was pride. Selena didn't want people to know that Dwight had run off and left her high and dry. In the beginning she really did think Dwight was missing until I told her about the other woman."

"What was the girl's name?"

"Susie Brinkman. She took a job with some oil company in Houston. That's all I know."

"Have you or Selena looked for Dwight in Houston?"

"Heavens, no. We want to keep a lid on this. If my clients found out that Dwight ran off with two hundred grand, they would beat a path to the bushes. No. No. This has got to be kept quiet for all our sakes. That's why Ginny needs to quit asking questions. I wish she'd just let things be," confessed Farley.

"But she doesn't know about this affair," I said.

Farley gave me a knowing look.

"She does? Well that . . . daughter of a dog. I'm sorry that I have bothered you with this. I could just kill Ginny." I got up and extended my hand.

Farley took it and we shook. "Let me walk you out."

"Thank you. I would appreciate that. Tell me. What happened to Dwight's secretary? I know they were close."

"Amanda didn't like the new position we offered, so she went to work for some big horse farm. She does all their paperwork. She's very good with details, you know. I gave her a glowing recommendation."

I stood at the office's front door. "Thank you, Farley. This conversation has been most illuminating."

"I knew that a woman with common sense like you would see the light. I hope you can convince Ginny that this is being handled in a way with the least confrontation or embarrassment to the family."

"I'll talk with her, I promise." I reached my hand up to his face. "Farley, it looks like you nicked yourself in the chin shaving."

Farley felt his chin and chuckled. "Did that falling off a rock pile when a kid. That scar's been there nearly as long as I have. No need to worry."

I gave him my sweetest smile. "I won't worry. You can count on that."

29

"I don't like gossiping," said Amanda, "and I don't like you bothering me at work."

"This is not gossiping. This falls under the umbrella of information gathering. If there is a possibility of Dwight being alive, Ginny ought to know. Now both Ginny and Farley Webb said you were close to Dwight. Do you think he is alive and living in Houston with a Susie Brinkman?"

Amanda grabbed my arm and pulled me into her office. "Sit down," she commanded. "Act like you are talking to me about a horse." She held out a book. "Point to some pictures and smile, for God's sake."

"What do you think?" I asked, thumbing through some catalog.

"I think that you are busybody getting me into trouble with my new boss."

"Come off it. Farley said he gave you a glowing recommendation when you quit."

Amanda snorted. "Oh, is that what Farley says? Farley fired me. Two weeks after Dwight goes missing, Farley says there's nothing for me at the company and he needs to let me go. Pronto."

"That's a far cry from his story."

"I don't give a hoot what his story is. I know the truth. I was asking too many questions about the spreadsheets after Dwight went missing. They didn't seem right to me."

"Farley accused Dwight of taking money."

"Oh, that's a laugh. Dwight was a straight arrow. I worked closely with that man for over five years. He was as honest as the day is long. If anything, Farley would be the one to dip his hand in the till."

"What do you think is going on, Amanda?"

"I think Farley is playing hanky-panky with the facts. I think he is using Dwight's disappearance to cover his tracks."

"Do you think Farley had anything to do with Dwight's disappearance?"

"He's too dumb or lazy to murder anyone. I don't think he had anything to do with that. No matter what his faults, Farley loved Dwight."

"Was Dwight having an affair with this Susie Brinkman?"

"I never saw any indication of it. That kind of stuff just permeates the air. Sooner or later everyone notices hot flashes going on between two people, but nobody noticed anything."

"Did Dwight seem unsettled to you?"

"Now that you mention it, Dwight seemed distant the last two weeks. I asked him what was wrong, but he said nothing."

"Do you think it had to do with the missing money?"

Amanda snorted. "Hell no. Dwight knew Farley. If he caught Farley taking out money, Dwight would just demand Farley pay it back or take a portion out of his check each month. That would not be a deal breaker for Dwight. He knew Farley's weaknesses and just learned to deal with him creatively over the years rather than force a confrontation. Farley was good at his job and brought in boatloads of money. It would have been replaced very quickly."

She pulled out another catalog and placed it before me. "I never got to finish working on the spreadsheets, but do you know how much was missing?"

"Farley says over two hundred thousand is gone and he told me that he believes Dwight took it to start a new life in Houston."

Amanda whistled. "Wow! That's a lot of cannoli. Has anyone checked in Houston for Dwight?"

"I think that's the next step."

"Let me know anything that you find out about Dwight. He was good to me. He was good to everybody."

I rose from the table. "Thanks for talking with me."

"I have Susie's cell phone number if you need it. Do you want it? She gave it to me before she left."

"What?"

Amanda scribbled a number on a Post-it and handed it to me.

I was stunned.

Could it be this easy?

Sometimes God does smile on me, wicked woman that I am.

30

I was very tired and on my way home to the Butterfly when I spied a dark blue sedan with tinted windows following two cars behind. Doing as I had been instructed, I turned into a convenience store parking lot.

Once inside the store, I called my daughter's cell phone. Once she answered, I sputtered, "Rosebud," and then hung up. I took my time buying junk food and then went to my car, wasting time eating the junk food. After twenty minutes had passed, I headed for the warehouse district on Old Frankfort Pike.

The area was going to be Lexington's new Bourbon and Entertainment district, but at the moment it was still full of empty warehouses and abandoned parking lots with no streetlights.

Glancing in the rearview mirror was the blue sedan, as I expected. Speeding up, I rushed through an opened gate into a rough parking lot that still had an intact fence. The sedan turned in after me.

Making sure my doors were locked, I had my Taser ready. Of course, these things were useless if my stalker had a gun, but I'd worry about that if I saw one.

The point was moot, for as soon as I gave the pre-arranged signal with my lights, four black SUVs sped out from behind buildings trapping the blue sedan inside the fence.

One man from each car jumped out with weapons drawn. The four surrounding the sedan yelled for the driver to turn off his car and come out with hands up.

Another SUV sped out from its hiding place and stopped near my car. Asa stepped out and knocked on my car window. "Are you okay?"

"Yes. Just exhausted. I thought he'd never catch up with me."

"We've been following him all day. He's been searching. It took him awhile to find you."

I got out and moseyed over to the sedan, knocking on the window. "You want to come out now?"

When he didn't emerge, I knocked harder. "I'm tired. My leg hurts. If you don't come out on your own, then these nice men are going to drag you out after I leave. What is done to you then will never be discussed with me. You get my drift?"

The car door slowly swung open and out stepped a sheepish Walter Neff with his hands held in the air.

"Walter. Walter. What are you up to?"

"Nothing. I was just going home and your thugs jumped me."

"They are not my thugs, Walter. They are Asa's thugs. You must know the rumors that Asa is not at all like me. I'm a softy. She is made of sterner stuff."

"I think social psychopath is the term that was used at the trial," deadpanned Asa, standing beside me.

I nodded in agreement. "Yes. I think that was the term."

We both stared at Walter.

Walter looked uncomfortably at Asa, who was holding a Glock 9 mm on him. After one of Asa's men frisked him, Walter asked, "Can I put my hands down now?"

Asa shrugged.

Walter slowly lowered his hands and tugged at his shirt collar. He glanced at one of Asa's men searching his ride.

"Why are you following me?" I asked.

"I told you. I was going home."

"Asa tells me that you and Fred O'nan are getting chummy."

"Who?"

"Now I know you think you have a beef with me over Ethel Bradley's lotto ticket, but you must realize that I didn't get any of the money either."

"Nobody did because you turned it over to that simpleton. I could have been rich."

"But it wasn't our lotto ticket." I took my cane and thumped Walter on the skull with it. "Look at your chest. There are four red lasers dancing on your nice black trench coat." I turned toward Asa. "Can I get a gun with one of those red light thingamabobs on it? They are so cool. Don't you think they're cool, Walter? Sorta gives you the heebie-jeebies when you see those lights flickering on your body, doesn't it. It would me."

Walter blinked while his hands twitched a little.

"Now, listen to me, Walter. I like you and don't want to see you get into trouble. You can either accept the fact the lotto ticket wasn't ours to keep or you can keep following me and feeding O'nan details of my whereabouts. But if you do, then my daughter, over whom I have no control . . ."

"And is a social psychopath," interjected Asa.

"Is going to let loose her 'thugs,'" I finished.

Walter shrugged. "I don't know who this O'nan is that you keep talking about."

Asa flipped on a recorder. Conversations between O'nan and Walter spilled into the darkening night.

"Okay. Okay. So I know the guy. So what?"

Asa stepped forward, invading Walter's personal space, causing him to back up against the sedan. "If you ever again follow my mother or put her in harm's way, then I am going to destroy your beautiful Avanti which you have hidden away in storage in Nicholasville and then I'm coming after you." She poked him on the chest. "When I catch up with you, I'm going to do to you what I did to the Avanti. Understand?"

Asa turned to me. "Mother, I'll take it from here."

I looked at Walter, who gave me a pleading stare. "Now, Asa, don't do anything crazy. I just wanted to give Walter a little tap on the shoulder. I don't think you need to break his jaw. Right, Walter?"

"Anything you say, Josiah. I'm your guy."

"I'm glad you see the light," growled Asa, "because now you're going to spill your guts about O'nan."

"What do you want to know?"

Asa beckoned to one of her men. He put away his gun and began pulling me toward my car.

"Asa. Asa! Don't do anything foolish," I cried out.

The hired gun turned on the car and slammed the door shut after pushing me in. "We'll take care of this, ma'am. You don't need to worry."

"Josiah, don't leave me alone with your daughter. Josiah. Josiah! Joooosiiiiah!"

I rolled down my window. "You brought this on yourself, Walter. Don't worry. She won't kill you. Not tonight anyway."

And with that statement, I was gone.

31

The next morning I got up early and let Baby with his pet cats outside to tinkle. Stumbling into the kitchen, I got Baby's breakfast ready while making a pot of tea. I just never developed a taste for coffee.

After putting Baby's food outside on the patio where he would share with his kitty cats, I went back to bed with a mug of hot tea laced with honey. After taking a few sips, I rolled over in bed and fell back asleep.

Unfortunately, it was not a restful sleep. I drifted into a recurring dream of O'nan pulling me off the cliff behind the Butterfly. The trauma always stayed with me. I would never get over the feeling of free-falling in space, reaching for anything that would belay my fall.

I could never parachute out of a plane or bungee jump off a bridge. I would never thumb my nose at gravity like others do. I appreciate Newton's law very much, thank you. I'm not that brave . . . or that stupid. Just thinking of it gives my stomach a queer ache.

My stomach had retained that same queer ache since Asa had played the tape of O'nan and Neff conspiring at Al's Bar.

Would O'nan never leave me alone?

How I wish to God I had never turned his name in for cheating on a test. Yes, I fib here and there, but there are some rules you don't cross and academic truthfulness is one.

But this thought keeps crossing my mind.

Did I really ruin O'nan's life? Or was I one of the few that put a STOP sign on his many cheats in life? Did he always hate me, or did seeing me again trigger some deep miasma that was below the surface just waiting to erupt?

I guess I would only know for sure when I met my Maker.

And I had the strong premonition that if O'nan had his way, it would be soon.

32

"Jeez, what happened to you, buddy-boy?"

"Asa Reynolds caught up with me. That's what happened."

O'nan pointed at Neff's swollen nose and black eyes. "She do that to ya?"

"I did it to myself while trying to run away from her. I tripped. You can say a car hood got between me and the ground. When I woke up, I was in an emergency room with a thousand dollars in my pocket with a note that the money was for the hospital bill. The car you loaned me was in the parking lot. Here are the keys."

O'nan quit smirking. "Whaddya doing?"

"Josiah and Asa Reynolds may be many things, but they're no cheats and they take whatever comes on the chin. No whining. Okay, Josiah whines a bit, but stops there.

"Asa could have left me in a ditch somewhere with a bullet hole in my head, but she took me to a hospital instead and even left money to pay for the bill." Neff held out the money. "I walked out, bandaged myself, and then came here."

Neff stepped closer while fingering the gun in his coat pocket . . . just in case O'nan tried something funny. "I'm done."

"We had a deal."

"Look, you stupid bastard, I don't want to do anything that hurts Josiah. I must have been out of my head with jealousy but I'm thinking straight now." Neff flung the car keys at O'nan.

"You can't walk out on me."

"Asa Reynolds has tapes of us talking at Al's Bar. I'm not going to prison for you, buddy-boy," sneered Neff. "You want Josiah Reynolds, then get her yourself."

Neff started to walk away, but stopped and turned. "I'll give you a piece of advice since you're so thick-skulled. If you want to get Josiah Reynolds, you'll have to take out Asa Reynolds first. Otherwise that daughter of hers will hunt you down until the end of her days." Neff laughed. "But the point is moot 'cause you couldn't take down a rabbit let alone those two broads. They're too tough."

Neff tugged at his coat collar against the cold wind. "Yep. I'd say those two are damned near invincible."

Laughing, Neff walked into the dark, leaving O'nan standing seething under a streetlight.

33

I was wrapping Christmas presents when Matt dragged the artificial tree out from its cupboard and began putting it together.

"With all the pine trees on this farm, we have this hideous aluminum job instead of a real Christmas tree."

"That tree is from the '50s and was my mother's," I reminded Matt.

He began assembling the motorized wheel that flashed four different colors onto the tree. "This thing belongs in a museum."

"And what a treat it is that we have it to ourselves."

Asa strode into the room. "That ugly thing again? Why can't we have a real Christmas tree instead of that ratty old thing?"

"I beg your pardon, little missy. My mother's tree is in mint condition. Matt, if you want a pine tree in your house, cut down anything on the farm you want. I've got plenty of ornaments you can use."

"Nah. Don't have the room. Besides, I like to complain about this tree. It's become a holiday tradition."

Franklin walked in from the kitchen with a bowl of popcorn. "I think it looks scrumptious. It's so mid-century. It's perfect for the Butterfly." He looked anxiously at the wrapped presents. "Are any of those for me? I hope. I hope. I hope. I hope."

I pushed one with my toe. "That one might have your name on it."

Franklin rushed to pick it up, but Asa beat him to it. She gave it a quick rattle.

"Stop it!" cried Franklin as he grabbed the package away from her. "You might break something."

Asa gave a short laugh. "I already know what it is and it's not breakable."

"Oh," pouted Franklin. "I was hoping it was a crystal bowl to match the vase I snatched from your mother. She knows how much I love that pattern. Waterford, isn't it?"

"Yes, it is and I want that vase back, Franklin," I complained as I fastened a bow to a superbly wrapped gift. The Japanese have nothing on me when it comes to beautifully wrapped gifts.

Franklin made a face. "We shall see."

"I'm done with my Christmas shopping. That was the last gift to wrap." I wiggled a little fanny jig in my chair.

"I haven't even started," moaned Asa.

"You don't need to get me anything, dear," I remarked.

"She says that every year and one year I actually believed her. I didn't get her a present," divulged Asa, grabbing a fist full of popcorn.

"Let me guess," drawled Matt. "She had a fit."

"Oh, you would have thought the Rapture had come and she'd missed it," laughed Asa. "I have never felt so guilty in my life. I'm still not over the trauma."

"I don't see how you could not get your only mother a Christmas gift," I remarked.

Asa threw up her hands. "See what I mean."

Matt started putting presents under the silver aluminum tree. "I think it has to do with you saying you didn't want anything."

"No one really means it when they say that. It's just what mothers do to look self-sacrificing. It's part of our shtick. But what we really want is for the children to make a big fuss. After the child is twenty-one, it's the parents who should get a little attention at Christmas," I admonished, glaring at Asa.

"Are we invited for Christmas dinner?" asked Franklin as he put away the wrapping paper and ribbons. "I'm not going home this year."

"Asa and I are going to the Big House for Christmas dinner. How about Christmas breakfast? We can eat and then open our presents."

"I guess that will have to do," whined Franklin.

"I'm inviting you all to my house for Christmas Eve. I'll have something edible and lots of champagne to make it go down if it's not," said Matt.

"Sounds great. Love to," I replied.

I noticed Asa studying my face. Her expression was soft as she came over and gave me a hug. "Thanks, Mom."

"Thanks for what?"

She shrugged. "For just making it. For not dying on me. For not giving up."

"I wouldn't think of it."

"Last Christmas you could barely walk or even talk. Now look at you."

"I didn't ever think I would want to live after that accident. The pain was so horrible, but I am here because of you, Asa." I looked at the three of them. "You all are so dear to me. Even you, Baby. Would someone get his big head out of the popcorn bowl?"

Matt held up his Coke can. "Here's to Josiah. Hoping for a pain free year."

"Hear. Hear," rejoined Franklin. He then stepped back to let Asa pass and inadvertently tripped over one of Baby's kitty cats, falling into the Christmas tree and knocking it over.

Rattled and gasping for air, Franklin reached for his Christmas gift and shook it close to his ear. "Ahhh, it's rattling now, Asa."

"That was an antique water bowl that had been part of the Lincoln estate," I wailed.

"Oh, no!" lamented Franklin. "What rotten luck." Downcast, he slumped on the couch, almost reduced to tears.

This is where I'm a stinker.

Franklin is a notorious gift hound. He likes to open his gifts when no one is around and then rewrap them. His real present was hidden in my closet while he was shaking a broken cheap candy dish, which I had planted as a decoy.

He looked so disheartened, I was tempted to tell him that he still had something special coming. But the temptation came and went.

After all, he stole my Waterford vase and if he was going to keep it, then Franklin was going to have to pay for it . . . with his misery.

I'm sure Jesus would never act this way, but then Jesus doesn't have to put up with Franklin on a daily basis.

I do.

34

Taking a deep breath, I dialed the number Dwight's secretary, Amanda, had given me for Susie Brinkman. To my surprise, I heard a cheerful "Hello?" on the other end.

"Hi, my name is Josiah Reynolds. I'm calling for the Dwight Wheelwright estate. Is this Susie Brinkman?"

"Wheelwright estate? Has something happened to Dwight? Oh God, no!" rushed the voice on the other end.

"Ms. Brinkman?"

"Yes, this is Susie. Has something happened to Dwight?"

"I'm sorry to tell you this, but Dwight has been missing for almost six months. Do you know where he is?"

There was a long silence on the phone.

"Ms. Brinkman. We are trying to talk to anyone that had a connection with Dwight. I understand that you worked with him."

I paused. "Farley Webb suggested that you were close to Dwight and that he might be living in Houston. If you could shed light on this, his family would be most grateful. All they want to know is if Dwight's alive. No one will bother him . . . or you. Ms. Brinkman? Ms. Brinkman!"

"Where are you?" she asked.

"Uhmmm. I'm at home."

"No, where are you calling from? What city?"

"Lexington," I told her.

"I'm at the Bluegrass Airport on a stopover for New York. Can you meet me here?"

I was so stunned that Susie was in Lexington that I was taken aback for a second. "Yes, I can be there in forty-five minutes."

"My plane leaves shortly after that. If you want to talk, you'd better hurry. I am wearing a gray pantsuit with a white silk top. I'll be in the downstairs lounge."

"Yes. Yes. I'll be there as soon as I can. Please don't leave until I talk with you. Goodbye." I rushed to find my city cane, car keys, and purse. "Baby, get out of the way!"

Slamming the door behind me, I gave it a tug, making sure it was locked. Rushing only made my limp more exaggerated. It was ugly to witness, but I had no choice. I had to get to the Bluegrass Airport and pronto!!!

35

I burned rubber, honey, and made it to the airport in record time. Swerving into a handicapped parking space, I was only fifty feet from the front doors.

Hurrying inside, I went to the lounge, which was packed with holiday travelers, and strained my neck looking for a gray pantsuit.

A pretty young blond thing waved at me. As I approached the table, she stood, motioning to the waitress. "Do you want anything?"

I was breathing heavily and ordered a Coke. Coke always seems to help my asthma.

She waited for me to collect myself, but kept looking at her watch. "I'm sorry. Your name again?"

"Just call me Josiah."

"I've got very little time. Let's hurry this along. You are telling me that Dwight is missing?"

"He went on a fishing trip in early July and never came home."

Tears welled in Susie's eyes at the mention of Dwight. She pulled a handkerchief from her purse and began dabbing her eyes. "So that's what happened. I always wondered."

I looked at Susie dumbfounded. "Are you telling me that Dwight is not with you?"

Susie shook her blond head. "Has everything been done to find him?"

"Yes."

"Does Selena think he's dead?"

"No," I replied, watching her closely. "She thinks he is with you, but she is pretending that he is missing."

She began to softly cry in earnest. Her shoulders shook. "I'm sorry. It's a shock to hear this, but I always wondered what had happened. I thought he had decided to stay with Selena. I called and called his cell phone, but he never picked up. Dwight didn't like confrontations and I thought he didn't want to tell me . . . oh well, it doesn't matter now." She looked up at me. "This is terrible but, oddly, I feel better about the situation now."

"Are you telling me that you and Dwight had a thing going on?"

Susie nodded and looked at me over her tear-soaked handkerchief. "We fell in love. Oh, Dwight had a horrible time with it. He loved Selena, but he was in love with me. We weren't on the make, you know. It happened innocently."

"Was Dwight to meet you in Houston?"

"Yes. Dwight finally made the decision to leave Selena. He was going to tell her in June but then she invited people to this huge birthday party before he could. Dwight decided to wait until after the party so as not to embarrass Selena in front of all their friends."

"I thought the party was his mother's idea."

"Oh, no. It was Selena's."

"Do you think she knew about the two of you and was trying to postpone the inevitable?" I asked.

"I don't know. We were very discreet, but I think Dwight told Farley about us when he took the money."

"The two hundred thousand dollars?" I asked, fishing.

"Yes. It was a down payment on Farley buying out Dwight. The rest of it was to be paid on a monthly installment for the next two years."

I sat back in my chair. "Really?"

Susie nodded. "I went ahead to Houston with the belief that Dwight would follow me as soon as he told Selena and straightened out his business affairs. It was to take only a week or so. He called me every day until July first. After that, I never heard from him again. I just thought he had a change of heart. I never dreamed that something had happened to him."

"Why Houston?"

"My family is there."

"May I ask why you are going to New York?"

"Business. Just for a day or two."

Susie looked at her watch. "I really must go. I have to go through security again, but I'm glad I talked with you. Will you please contact me if something comes up? I need to know."

"Yes. I promise," I offered, watching her leave.

She wasn't pulling a suitcase.

I sat at the table nursing my Coke, studying on what she had said when I realized the waitress had handed me the tab. "Well, that little fart," I complained. "She stuck me with the bill for her drink."

And I had left my purse in the car.

Great!

36

After talking the waitress out of calling security, I rushed to my car, got my purse, and came back to pay the tab. I could see that she forgave me for all the fuss after I gave her a big tip.

I then limped over to the flight status board stationed before the security area. There indeed was a flight from Houston with a stopover period before heading to New York.

Since I was not allowed to go to the gates, I had to content myself with that. I really wanted to see if Susie got on that plane.

Standing in the airport looking at the flight board, I knew three things.

1. Susie would be boarding a new plane.
2. I knew that there were no lockers in the waiting areas after you got through security.
3. I also knew that business people always took carry-ons onto the plane themselves. It was too risky to check bags.

So where was Susie's luggage?

37

"So you knew?"

"I don't believe it. I never believed it," defended Ginny.

"How did you find out?"

"Selena told me, but I don't believe it."

"Yeah, I got that. How did she know?" I asked.

"She said that Farley told her that Dwight had probably run off with another woman. But Jo, he would never abandon his little girl. Never. I know my son."

I didn't know what to say. I just knew that I was mad. Ginny had used me and had not been honest.

Ginny inhaled deeply from a cigarette and nervously tapped the kitchen table.

I waved away the smoke. "Ginny, I'm out of my depth here. I don't who's lying, and you have not been completely truthful with me. You should have told me about the rumors."

A pink flush ran up Ginny's neck to her cheeks. "I asked for a copy of the check for this two hundred thousand dollars that Dwight supposedly cashed."

"Farley inferred that Dwight had stolen the money. There was never any mention that Farley was buying Dwight out. But this Ms. Brinkman said Dwight wanted to be bought out. So you see that I am just going round and round in circles. I have no authority to make Farley open the company's books. You really need to talk to the police. I think there is enough to re-open the investigation."

"I've tried and tried. You were my last hope to shake something loose."

"I'm sorry but there's nothing more I can do."

Ginny took a puff. "I see. Well, if there's nothing more . . ."

Getting the hint, I stood. "I'll let myself out."

I felt bad, really bad, leaving Ginny alone, smoking at a dirty kitchen table and drinking stale coffee.

But it was over.

Until Dwight surfaced one way or the other, there was nothing anyone could do.

38

"I don't see why you feel so guilty. You went as far as you could until the trail went cold," Asa said.

"Ginny was one of the few people who stuck by me when your father left."

"Deserted us, you mean."

"Left. Let's not be so dramatic."

"Whatever you say, Mother."

I gave Asa one of those maternal looks. "I wanted to repay her kindness to both of us. She got guff from people because she stood by me . . . and you."

"Has she paid for the lab testing and your gas money?"

"Not yet, but she will when she can."

Asa gave me a doubtful look.

I shook my head in weariness. I was exhausted both mentally and physically. And I still had Christmas breakfast to do in a couple of days. I was beginning to wonder if I was up to it.

Recognizing the signs that I was plumb worn out, Asa took the reins. "Okay, Mommy Dearest, it's time you went to bed."

"I've got things to prepare for the breakfast."

"No, you don't. I'm going to call Franklin and we are going to handle breakfast. He's got nothing else to do. We are going to have a simple breakfast of eggs, country ham, pastries, fruit, and that's all."

"Matt wanted waffles too."

"I'll have Franklin pick up some frozen waffles at the store."

"That's simply won't do for Matt. He'll want homemade."

"It will have to. He'll understand, Mom."

"What about the house?"

"What about it? Eunice and Amelia have this house so clean I literally could eat off the floor."

"There's laundry to do, flower arrangements, and the table needs to be set."

"I'll take care of everything. This is one of my presents to you. You need to rest. I mean really rest. And to make sure that you do, I will throw in a bonus.

"One of my guys is staying in town for the holidays. I will have him follow this Farley Webb and see what this guy is up to."

"That is what I wanted, but was afraid to ask."

"There's a catch, though. He's alone for the holidays. Can we invite him to Matt's Christmas Eve dinner and our breakfast?"

"I insist upon it. This is wonderful. I can really sleep, knowing that someone is still digging."

I gave Asa a kiss and called to Baby.

But Baby was preoccupied looking out the glass patio doors for his kitty cats.

They were late this evening. If they didn't come in soon, Asa would have to walk to the barn and check on them.

It was snowing now.

I could tell she wanted them inside before the snow got too deep or too slick. It was not unusual for us to have ice storms without warning. It made getting around outside very tiresome.

"Go on, Mom. I'll see about the cats. The rest of the animals have been fed and watered."

I gave her a brief smile as I trotted off to bed, leaving Asa and Baby peering through the glass door at the distant tobacco barn for the cats.

My last thought was of Brannon, my late husband as a young man, wishing he were spending Christmas with us. Smiling, I fell asleep.

39

I awoke with a start. You know that kind of waking as if you had been drowning—that slow struggle through thick water, then gasping as you finally shoot beyond the confines of the water into the open air.

Glancing at the illuminated clock next to the bed, I could see it was just after three.

Switching on the light proved that Baby was not in his bed. Perhaps he was sleeping with Asa, but there were no signs of the cats. Even if the majority were with Asa, one or two would have been curled up with me.

Concerned, I climbed out of bed and went into the hallway.

There were quite a few lights in the house left on, not the usual button-down that one does when going to bed.

The Butterfly didn't feel right.

A tingling traveled up my spine.

Asa's bedroom door was open.

I stood at the doorway, feeling for the light switch. She wasn't in bed.

Nor was there any sign of Baby. By now, Baby would have heard me and have been by my side, seeing what I was up to and wondering if it involved food.

"Baby! Asa!" Hope against hope, I would have been thrilled to find them both on the couch in the living room, having drifted off to sleep. But no one returned my call.

"Dear Lord," I muttered. Hurrying throughout the house, I checked every room, but no sign of Asa, the dog or the cats.

My heart was racing now.

Going to the small room by the front door, I started turning on all the screens for the cameras that monitored the Butterfly and the farm. With a press of a few buttons, I could turn lights on all over the farm and use a joystick to move the cameras stationed at strategic points.

Outside it was snowing, making visibility difficult. Some of the camera's screens were dusted white.

I jostled the joystick so I could see the ground near the front door. There were human and dog footprints leaving the house. I followed those tracks all the way to the tobacco barn, which had been turned into a stable.

Asa had gone to gather the cats, but never returned.

I shot a look behind me as I heard whimpering. I realized it was me making those sounds.

Frantically, I checked the bee yard. The snow did not look disturbed and the hives were blanketed in snow.

I checked the front entrance to the farm. There were tire tracks, but they could be from Matt's car. Checking all the other camera sites, I didn't find any more footprints nor signs of my daughter.

Pushing the buttons for every light on the farm, I lit the joint up like the Fourth of July.

My hands were shaking so I could barely push Matt's numbers on the phone.

"Hello? This better be good," responded a groggy voice.

"Matt. Matt. Get up. Something's wrong. Asa and Baby are not in the house. There're footprints going into the old tobacco barn. Help me."

"What?"

"Matt, wake up. I think there's trouble. Meet me at the stable."

Matt was suddenly alert. "You stay there. I'll go check."

"No, don't go alone. I'm calling Charles. Wait for me to pick you up." I put down the phone.

Throwing on an overcoat along with some boots, thick gloves and an old hat, I knew I looked a sight but didn't care.

Suddenly remembering I hadn't called Charles, I anxiously dialed the number of his house on Lady Elsmere's farm.

He picked up on the first ring. "What's wrong?"

I quickly told him that Asa and Baby were not in the house.

"I'll meet you at the stable." Then a click and the dial tone.

Grabbing the car keys and the sycamore cane that Moshe Goren had carved for me, I flung open the door and hurried to the Prius.

It didn't take me very long to get to Matt's little house. He was waiting outside. "Let me drive," he suggested. I changed seats.

The snow was coming down more heavily.

Matt switched on the windshield wipers.

It took us only a few moments to get to the converted tobacco barn, but it seemed like hours. As soon as the car stopped, I jumped out.

Charles, with several of his grandsons, was already standing in front of the barn studying the footprints at the entrance. The front double doors were slightly pulled apart.

"Asa," I called. "Asa!"

Barking.

"That's Baby," I cried to the others. "Baby. Baby!" I rushed into the darkness.

Charles followed me with a flashlight while Matt felt for the light switch.

Immediately the barn was flooded with light. I started opening all the stalls.

The retired racehorses calmly chewed on hay, as were several little goats. In another stall, the peacocks, angry at being disturbed, hissed when I opened their little cubicle.

A llama reached over through the slats and nipped my shoulder.

"Josiah, over here," called Charles.

Matt and I rushed over to Charles. In an empty stall lay Asa with Baby guarding. Upon seeing us he growled, baring his teeth.

While Mastiffs rarely bite, they will if they feel threatened. An English Mastiff's bite is 550-660 lbs per square inch, while a lion's bite is 680 lbs PSI. See what I'm talking about.

They were bred in Britain two thousand years ago to hunt and protect. Julius Caesar is said to have brought this ancient breed from Britain to Rome to fight in the arena games.

Behind me, I heard Charles on his walkie-talkie telling one of his daughters to bring the dart gun and the Hummer with the emergency kit.

"The gun won't be necessary," I said.

"That dog's an English Mastiff. He has had centuries of breeding to make him instinctively guard his master. You know that they had to be put down to get to their wounded or dead masters during the Crusades. He's no different. It's in their blood to defend until death." Charles swirled me around to face him. "I'm just gonna tranquilize him."

"But Asa's not Baby's master. I am." I pulled away from Charles and stepped into the cubicle.

Baby bared his teeth and snapped at the air, giving me a warning.

"Baby. Baby. It's me. It's Mommy," I cooed.

One of the grandsons moved.

Baby lunged forward and would have bitten my hand if I hadn't moved quickly enough.

"You all move back. You're making him nervous. Step back where Baby can't see you," I demanded.

Baby stood quivering in front of Asa's prone body. I decide another tact. "BABY! Lie down. Lie down. I need to see to Asa." I gave the hand signal to Baby to lie down, making sure his good eye saw it. "It's me. Josiah. Baby, do as I tell you. LIE DOWN!" I held out my hand so Baby could smell me.

Baby stretched his neck to sniff. He gave a little yelp of recognition, moving toward me. As always, he leaned his two hundred-plus pounds against my bad leg.

I scratched behind his ears. "Good Baby. Good Baby. I tied a rope through his collar, while continuing to praise him. "It's okay. It's okay."

Charles' daughter, Amelia, had joined us and handed me a bloody piece of meat through one of the stall slats. "It's been doctored with a tranquilizer. It will make him relax."

I looked at the meat without enthusiasm.

"Don't worry, Josiah. It won't hurt him. Just makes him sleepy. I've already called the vet. I'll stay with Baby until he comes."

Reluctantly, I took the meat and held it out to Baby. "Here, Baby. Eat this."

Baby sniffed it, while looking at me for guidance. "It's okay, Baby. You can eat it. You've done your job. Treat. Treat."

At the suggestion of a treat, Baby snatched the meat from my hand and consumed it in several gulps.

I was lucky that I still had my fingers intact.

"Everyone go to the other side of the barn," I requested.

Quietly they retreated as I slowly pulled on the rope, leading Baby into an empty stall. As I closed the door to the stall, Baby looked at me in confusion. "You did good, Baby. Good dog. Good dog."

Baby's eyelids were starting to droop. The medication was already working.

Behind me, I heard Charles and Matt rush to Asa.

"She's alive," called out Matt. After checking for broken bones, Matt swooped up Asa and carried her to the Hummer, which was waiting to take her to the hospital.

Charles' other daughter, Bess, was already inside the car putting blankets on Asa while Charles took the wheel.

I hopped inside.

Within minutes, we were flying down the road to the nearest emergency room while Matt and the grandsons waited for the police.

"That barn must be cursed," I muttered to no one in particular. "This is the second bloodletting in it."

"What's that?" asked Bess.

"Just thinking out loud," I replied while holding Asa's hand. "Asa, wake up. Talk to me." I gave her a little shake. "Asa!"

Asa slowly opened her eyes. "I could be dead, but I would still hear that irritating voice coming from beyond the vale."

Grinning, I replied, "You can't be that dead if you are using phrases like 'beyond the vale.' "

Asa gave a little smile, more like a smirk. "I heard everything that went on with Baby. It took you long enough to find me." She paused. "Everything is spinning. I'm going to sleep now."

"No you're not," commanded Bess. "You're going to stay awake." She gave Asa a vicious pinch.

"Ouch! That hurt," mumbled Asa.

"Good. Now keep talking."

"What happened?" I questioned.

"Went to check on the cats. Someone jumped me from behind." She snorted. "Speaking of behinds, I think Baby got a piece of *their* behind."

"No pun intended."

Asa softly chuckled.

Suddenly the Hummer stopped and the car doors were flung open. A doctor and several nurses put Asa on a gurney and rushed her into the emergency room.

Bess had an orderly bring a wheelchair. I really was in no shape to walk at this point. Between the pain and adrenaline, I was trembling so that I could barely negotiate my way out of the Hummer, even with help.

She wheeled me into the waiting room where I started my vigil of waiting for the doctor.

It seemed like forever.

40

O'nan unwrapped the bandage from his hand. It looked pretty nasty. Tenderly, he examined his hand. He was sure it was broken. That damn dog. It came out of nowhere.

He was going to need antibiotics and have his hand set. Maybe even surgery. What was he going to do?

Going to a hospital would be admitting his guilt. The DA would subpoena his medical file and that would be that. He would go to jail for assault and battery. The charge might even be attempted murder if Neff testified.

A wave of pain shot through O'nan. He vomited into the bathroom sink.

Wiping his face, he thought of the doctor at the Ephraim McDowell hospital in Danville whom he had caught with an underage girl when he was still a cop.

O'nan had let him go, as the girl stated that she had lied about her age, but still . . . a rumor like that could ruin a doctor's promising career.

And O'nan still had the guy's phone number.

41

Kelly stuck his head in the door. "Hey there," he said, looking concerned at Asa. "How's it going?"

"How did you know?" asked Asa, struggling to sit up in her hospital bed.

Kelly grimaced. "I'm a cop. What do you mean–how do I know?"

I started to get up to leave.

Kelly waved for me to sit back down. "Can't stay long. The kids are waiting in the hall. We were doing some late Christmas shopping when I heard the chatter over the scanner. Just wanted to see how you were."

I could see that Asa was disappointed. "Doing fine. They had me overnight for observation. I think as soon as the doctor comes for her rounds, she might let me go."

Kelly glanced at me. "I'm sure you're relieved."

"Very. Thank goodness Baby was with her."

"What happened? Do you know who the perp is?"

Asa shook her head. "He came from behind. Must have hit me with a shovel. I was in and out. I heard Baby rush him and then some screaming. After that I blacked out entirely until Mom found me."

"We know who did this," I blurted out. "Why don't you guys pick him up?"

"Can't find O'nan. Supposedly he's in Florida spending Christmas with some relatives."

"Unbelievable," I seethed.

"The Florida boys are going to check on him for us. The judge gave him permission to go."

"Unbelievable," I said again.

A little boy popped his head into the room. "DAD! We gotta go. The stores are gonna close soon."

"Be right there, son. Go wait out in the hallway." Kelly looked apologetically at us.

There was an uneasy silence among the three of us for a moment.

"I best be going," Kelly finally said.

Asa nodded.

"Let me know how you're doing?"

"Sure thing."

Kelly started to leave and then swung around. "Merry Christmas, Asa."

"Same to you, Kelly."

He gave Asa a look of longing and regret before walking out.

After peeking at Asa's crestfallen face, I knew the affair was over.

It was for the best, but that fact didn't make it any less painful.

My daughter had caught on fire.

42

I was determined this Christmas was not going to be a gloomy affair. It was solemn enough last year with me drinking soup through a straw because my jaws were wired shut.

Going though a dusty box in my office, I found some old paraphernalia from a dinner party I gave years ago. Taking some paper towels, I dusted off my treasures and put them on everyone's plate.

Then I called Franklin and told him to come early to set up the video camera for me. I wanted a record of our happy event.

For obvious reasons, we had skipped Matt's Christmas Eve party.

Asa just hadn't felt up to it.

Franklin told me with glee that it had been a total bore with a lot of anal lawyers attending. Even Matt thought the conversation was tedious.

"Without my presence," Franklin stated, "it would have been a total disaster." According to Franklin, he had been the life of the party.

I called Eunice, who was with Shaneika and Linc in Florida for the holidays. Also Shaneika's Thoroughbred, Comanche, was with them in training. According to Eunice, his time was faster and Shaneika had entered him in some races. If he did well, she would bring him home to race at Keeneland. The goal was to get him ready for the Kentucky Derby.

Eunice stated that she would be back sometime in the middle of January.

I wished her a Merry Christmas and hung up. I didn't tell her about Asa. There was no need to cast a shadow over her happiness.

Looking at the clock, I saw that it was already ten. Guests were to arrive very soon and I still had to dress.

The doorbell rang. I hurried to the front door, pushing a cat off the dining room table on the way. I made a mental note to replace a plate, as the cat was sitting with his furry fanny squarely on my good china.

"Baby, get your friends together or out they go," I threatened as I opened the door.

Franklin pushed his way in with his arms full of presents. "Merry Christmas, good lady," he yelled. "Merry Christmas, Baby! God bless us everyone!"

"Welcome, Tiny Tim. Where's Bob Cratchit?" I asked, looking out the door.

Baby responded to Franklin's greeting by sticking his snout in Franklin's crotch.

"That's a little too friendly there, doggy pal of mine," giggled Franklin. "Here, help me with these."

He dumped some packages into my arms.

I placed them under the tree. "I've got to get dressed. Can you make sure the cats don't get on the table?"

"Why don't we put them out?"

"Uhmmm, Baby would have a fit."

"Oh, I see. Baby is running this house." He petted Baby, who had followed him into the great room. "So you're really the one to suck up to."

"Franklin!"

"Yes, I'll watch the cats," he sighed as he began rearranging the ornaments on my Christmas tree.

I hurried to change into a simple but gorgeous silk lounging gown. Of course, Franklin had picked it out for me. It took me much longer to do my makeup. My right hand was shaking. I kept smearing lipstick on my upper lip. Once presentable, I made a grand entrance.

Most everyone was present.

Asa was wearing her usual black.

I patted her on the shoulder and said, "Thanks for dressing up. You look so cheerful. Are you going to sing a dirge for us later on?"

Asa sniffed and tossed her dark hair. She hated me commenting on her clothes, which usually resembled

Batgirl's, but that didn't stop her from always commenting on mine.

"And who are you?" I asked a young man also dressed in black and standing by Asa's side.

"My name is Boris. I work for Asa," he stated in a thick Eastern European accent. "Thank you for having me."

"My pleasure. I hope you enjoy our simple fare."

Franklin bounced to my side with a tray of glasses filled with champagne. "I see Natasha and Boris are attending." (For those too young to remember or just don't know cool pop culture icons, Natasha and Boris were cartoon criminals/spies on the Rocky and Bullwinkle show 1961-1964.)

"None for me. Thanks," murmured Asa.

Boris shook his head.

Franklin gave me a look, muttering "killjoys" and buzzed away to the front door as the doorbell rang. In marched June and Matt, both accepting glasses of champagne from Franklin.

June glimmered with all the diamonds she wore.

And Matt shimmered like a god with his dark good looks.

He never failed to take my breath away.

Matt looked like the '50s matinee movie idol Victor Mature, who was from Louisville. Noted for acting with his forehead, Mature was once asked if he was bothered playing Samson's father in a TV remake of Mature's epic film *Samson and Delilah,* as he had played the virile Samson years before. Mature said, "If the money's right, I'd play his mother."

Behind Matt, straggled in Charles dragging a little red wagon full of gifts.

"Charles, how wonderful," I gushed. "You changed your mind about joining us." I peered around him, looking for the rest of his family.

"We're busy cooking for tonight. Now don't fill up too much because we've got a big dinner coming. We're cooking what we want to eat, not that hoity-toity food she orders," grinned Charles, thumbing at June.

June rolled her eyes and made straight for Asa's companion. "Who are you?"

"My name is Boris," he replied haltingly.

June patted him on the arm. "Of course, you are."

"Boris, this is Lady Elsmere," introduced Asa.

"Just call me June," insisted her Ladyship. She winked at Asa. "Salut," she murmured before downing her champagne. "Oh, my dears, you don't have any bubbly."

"We're not having any," replied Asa.

June snapped her fingers at Franklin, who rushed over with filled glasses. She took several and handed them to Asa and Boris. "You don't have to drink. Just pretend you're having a good time." Then she took two glasses for herself. "Killjoys," she murmured under her breath.

"That's what I said," confided Franklin as they strode away.

Asa burst out laughing at Boris' confused expression. "Don't expect sanity here. Kentucky is known for its eccentrics."

"Eccentrics?"

"Kooks, my dear Boris. Crazies."

"Ah, crazies. Yes."

I made a Screwdriver and took it to Boris. "You'll like this better."

Boris sniffed it suspiciously.

"It's got vodka in it."

Boris shook his head and handed the glass back to me. "I don't like vodka. Thank you."

"Hell has certainly frozen over," I quipped.

"What?" asked Boris.

"Oh, Mother is commenting on her stereotypical idea of Eastern Europeans."

"If a Kentuckian was a guest in your home, wouldn't you offer him bourbon first?" I replied, defending myself. "Let's try this. Boris, what would you like to drink?"

"Tomato juice."

"Coming right up." I asked Franklin to get Boris a virgin Blood Mary.

"Everyone. Let's sit down."

"No presents first?" complained Franklin.

"Franklin, you're just like a kid," commented Matt.

"What's wrong with that?" replied Franklin. "You act like an old man."

"Be nice, children," I remarked. "We have so many things to be thankful for."

"Like?" asked Franklin.

"Well, I made it another year," laughed June.

"To the Queen of Lexington," we all said, lifting our glasses in concordance.

I continued. "I'm doing much better. My therapy is almost at its end. I feel pretty good most of the time. Asa is with us and not stuck in some dreary hospital. We have a new friend, Boris. And Matt has a baby on the way."

Everyone clapped.

Baby thumped his giant head on the table, licking the tablecloth.

"And Baby has just four more months of being a puppy." I kissed the top of his massive head.

Baby panted and swallowed a great amount of drool.

"If it wasn't for Baby, I wouldn't be here," remarked Asa. She stood holding up a glass of water. "Here's to Baby."

We all stood and saluted Baby.

After we sat back down, I made everyone put on the paste diamond tiaras and wave the wands I had placed on their plates. I even had a tiara for Baby, which he loved. Even the manly Boris got silly and wore his headpiece.

Christmas breakfast lasted until early afternoon. Finally, Matt took Lady Elsmere home, along with Franklin, who squeezed an invitation to nap in one of the guest rooms at the Big House until dinner.

Boris agreed to stay. Asa showed him to a guest bedroom to rest while I headed for my room.

I needed to digest my breakfast to make room for Charles' Christmas dinner. I intended to eat until I could barely roll myself home . . . or I popped.

43

Old fashioned chicken and dumplings, baked ham topped with pineapple and cherries, macaroni and cheese, turnip greens, mashed potatoes smothered with gravy, fried corn, candied yams, carrot raisin salad, apple pear salad, cranberry sauce, dinner rolls and cornbread, gobs of butter, sweet potato pie and pound cake with bourbon hard sauce.

"What is this?" asked Boris, pointing to the hard sauce.

Amelia replied, "It's a Southern topping for cakes and pies. It's made with powdered sugar, melted butter, and as much bourbon as you can stand whipped into a thick cream. Here's a spoonful. See if you like it."

Boris licked a bit of the topping from the spoon. "Whew, that is strong," he gushed, looking at Asa.

Asa smiled back. "Come on. You sit by me."

At Lady Elsmere's Christmas dinner, there was no employee or employer. Just family. There wasn't even a Lady Elsmere, just June from Monkey's Eyebrow.

June motioned for her nephew, Tony, to sit down with his valet, Giles.

"Where are the seating cards?" asked Tony incredulously.

"Just sit your butt down anywhere," ordered June.

Bess put the last bowl on the table and sat between her father, Charles, and her son, who pushed in her chair.

June looked around. "Everyone here?"

Charles nodded.

June bowed her head. "Dear Lord, thank you for everyone being together and in good health. Thank you for our wonderful friendships and all the good grub. Amen." She looked up, grinning. "Let's eat, children."

Everyone grabbed the bowl in front of them, piled food on their plate and then passed the bowl to the left. It was a noisy affair with everyone talking and laughing at once.

An hour later we were in the library in front of a large fire, admiring June's Christmas tree that reached the top of the fourteen-foot ceiling.

There was also a beautiful silver menorah on the fireplace mantel.

June pointed to it. "My good friend, Rabbi Geffen, is coming this week for tea. I wanted him to feel at home."

"He'll appreciate the gesture," I assured.

"Here's something for you," she said, handing me a beautifully wrapped box.

"You didn't have to, but I'm glad you did," I kidded as I opened the box. "Oh, June. I can't accept this. It's too much."

June closed my fingers over a diamond brooch in the shape of a butterfly. "I won't be here much longer, Josiah. It's time to let go of things so others can enjoy them. This is the first piece of jewelry my first husband bought me when he made his money. It's special to me. I want you to have it."

Hearing ooohs and ahhhs in the room, I turned to see others opening their gifts from June. Each woman had received a piece of jewelry from June's fabulous collection.

Asa held up a yellow diamond ring encircled with tiny white diamonds.

Bess and Amelia were trying on their pearl necklaces while Charles' wife admired an antique emerald and diamond necklace and matching ring that had supposedly belonged to Josephine Bonaparte.

In the corner I heard Franklin frantically opening his small box whispering, "God, oh God. Please let it be bling." He ripped open the box and shouted, "Thank you, June!" Happily, he shoved on a gentleman's diamond pinky ring and showed it to Matt.

June shook her head. "Maybe you should have him tested."

I laughed.

The rest of the men cautiously opened theirs. Charles' grandsons got checks for college. They must have been a large sum, as they were grinning from ear to ear.

Matt got a gift card to spend on items needed for the coming baby.

Tony and his valet, Giles, also got gift cards. The valet mumbled thanks to June, while Tony just stuck the card in his coat pocket as an afterthought.

Charles strummed through an old leather bound book. "My goodness, what is this?"

"It is one of Henry Clay's diaries in which he writes about your great, great grandmother suing him for her freedom. Here's the provenance," she pointed. June looked kindly at Charles. "I thought you might like to have this since it's about your family before the Civil War."

"Here, let me take it before you cry all over the leather," said Charles' wife as she carefully put the diary back in the box.

"I don't know what to say," gasped Charles.

"Does it make you happy, Charles?" asked June.

"It sure does. It's a part of my family's past. It's part of me."

"No more needs to be said." June affectionately patted Charles' hand.

Matt put a new log on the fire and offered to freshen everyone's drinks.

"I can't accept this," said Boris to Asa, referring to his gift card.

"You will offend June if you don't take it," replied Asa, admiring her new diamond ring on her left hand. She raised her hand to show it to Boris.

Boris was standing in front of the glass double doors that lead out to the pool patio. Beyond the pool, one could see the roof of the Butterfly.

Asa saw something flicker behind him. Rushing to the glass doors, she screamed, "MOM! THE BUTTERFLY IS ON FIRE!"

44

Asa hurriedly punched in the code to the front door. Hearing the click, I pushed open the door only to have Baby rush me, and the cats leap across the threshold to hurry toward the barn.

I checked Baby while Asa ran into the house. Holding Baby's collar, I stepped inside the house and sniffed the air. No smoke.

Outside I could hear the men putting ladders on the roof and opening the hoses. In the distance I could hear the wail of a fire truck.

I flipped a light switch. The electricity was still on. I checked the land phone. It was still working.

Asa came back with her gun holster on. "All the doors are locked. The windows are closed. I checked every room. There's no sign of fire."

Sighing relief, I let go of Baby, which was a bad idea because he went directly outside and started harassing everyone who was trying to put the fire out on the roof.

Asa put him on a leash and tapped his nose with her index finger when he wouldn't listen. He hated to be reprimanded and sat in sulky silence. He had been having a wonderful time.

Matt and Boris climbed down the ladders looking disheveled. Boris shook his head at Asa. Charles and his grandsons finished surveying the immediate grounds of the house as his daughters began raking up the debris that Matt had pulled off the roof.

As Matt and Boris came up to us, Franklin drove up from checking on Matt's house. "All clear," Franklin said, getting out of his Smart car. "House is perfect."

"What's going on?" I asked.

"It looks like someone put debris on top of the roof and then set it on fire," replied Matt, staring at the rooftop.

Charles and his grandsons hurried to our little group huddled in the driveway. "Look what we found," announced Charles, showing us an empty gas can.

"Why would anyone do that? What's the purpose?" I mulled.

Boris shrugged. "For a diversion?" he suggested.

Asa snapped her head up. "June and your wife, Charles. They're alone in the Big House."

"Tony and Giles are there with them," responded one of the grandsons.

"And you trust those limeys with our women!"

shouted Charles. "Get back in the cars. Something's not right."

I put Baby back in the house, locked the front doors and drove back to June's with Franklin. We were the last to arrive.

Rushing into the Big House, I found everyone in the library with Asa and Boris pointing guns at Tony and his man, Giles aka Liam Doyle, as they reached for the sky.

June and Charles' wife were sitting quite calmly in green leather chairs near the fire, sipping brandy. There was a derringer in June's lap and a twinkle in her eyes.

The derringer would explain a teenage boy bleeding on her expensive oriental carpet and the twinkle would explain the thrill of shooting the teenager.

"That crazy old bitch shot me!" exclaimed the youth.

"Just be glad I shot you in the leg, young man," said June.

"And that other bitch tried to cave my head in with a poker."

June looked at Charles' wife. "Mrs. DuPuy, being of a darker persuasion, (pronounced per-swaaay-shion) doesn't like white males pointing guns at her."

"I don't like *anyone* pointing a gun at me. I don't care what color," scolded Mrs. DuPuy, pointing a finger at the boy. "It was very rude of you." She looked up wide-eyed at us. "He tried to steal Josephine's jewels. We just couldn't allow that," she stated matter of factly.

"So I shot him," drawled June.

"That was after I tried to crack his head open with the poker," concurred Mrs. Dupuy.

"It's just a flesh wound," claimed Boris, examining the bullet wound. "Put a band aid on it and he will be fine."

"I'm in pain," whined the boy.

"But why are Tony and Giles standing with their hands up in the air?" I asked.

"Because Mr. Tony tried to yank my necklace off after the boy was shot," said Mrs. Dupuy.

"That makes us think that he might have had something to do with this," claimed June.

"I was just trying to help," spat Tony at Mrs. DuPuy. She snorted in derision.

Boris kicked the boy's bad leg. "Tell us what's up or you're going to prison for long time."

"That man paid me one hundred dollars if I was to set fire to that weird house down yonder," the boy confessed, pointing to Tony. "And I was to get five hundred more if I robbed this house. I was to steal a green and white necklace. The one that lady's wearing," he added.

"I've never seen this boy before in my life," Tony scoffed, looking annoyed.

"Six hundred dollars to steal necklace worth millions?" uttered Boris.

"Boy, you've been had," remarked Charles. He sat by his wife. "I hear the fire trucks." Turning to his grandsons, he ordered, "One of you go down to the Butterfly and tell them to come up here. Let them through the side property gate. We've got an injured boy."

"I had nothing to do with this!" protested Giles. "I didn't know anything about it."

"Shut up!" demanded Tony.

"I'm not going to prison for you. I like it here. I like my room. I like the food. I like the bourbon." Giles turned toward June. "Lady Elsmere, I'd nothing to do with this. I will do anything to stay. Help Charles around the house. I'll even shovel shi… horse poop if you will let me stay. I'm begging you. I've got nowhere else to go."

"Tony, did Giles have any prior knowledge of your little faux pas?" asked June. "Don't bother to deny it. This has your fingerprints all over it. Think of the English gentleman's code before you speak."

Tony considered for a moment. "No."

Giles looked relieved.

June picked the derringer off her lap and pointed it at Tony. "Everyone leave the room but Tony and this boy. Stall the firemen and the police. Now scoot."

Before I left the room, I asked, "Where did you get the derringer?"

June grinned. "In my décolletage, where all ladies of quality keep their weapons."

"Always?"

"Always."

"Just when you think you know someone." I left the room, shutting the door quietly behind me. Of course, everyone was standing in the hallway straining to hear.

Franklin brought glasses so we could amplify our hearing with our ears pressed against the bottom of the glasses that were pressed against the door.

Boris asked, "What's she saying? I don't understand her English."

"Shush!" went everyone.

Charles put down his glass. "She's going old school country girl on them. There's no Lady Elsmere there. Just June Webster from Monkey's Eyebrow."

"Those words even make me blush. Salty isn't the word," stated Franklin.

Asa looked at me. "Mother, what's a . . .?"

"Hush. I'll tell you when we get home."

Mrs. DuPuy could no longer hold off the firemen and the police.

The authorities tramped down the hallway, scattering our little party. They were in no mood for our silliness.

I didn't blame them for being in a bad mood. We had gotten them out on Christmas Day.

Charles and his wife hurried to the kitchen to fix them something to eat. That would certainly take the edge off their foul humor.

After coming out of the library looking confused, but elated at the promise of a large donation to their favorite charity by Lady Elsmere, the police waited until the boy was ensconced in an ambulance and then took off without taking our statements. The firemen, loaded with baskets of food and wine, happily returned to their fire station.

Matt gave Asa, Boris, and me a ride home. Matt and Franklin went back to Matt's place with Franklin still showing his pinky ring to Matt every five seconds.

"Boris, can you stay tonight?" I asked. I knew if he didn't stay, Asa would be up all night guarding. She needed to get some sleep.

"Yes. I've got my gear in the SUV."

"I feel very blessed tonight," I confessed to Asa.

"How can you say that, Mom?"

"No one got seriously hurt. The fire didn't damage the house. You and I got some fabulous bling. And June got to shoot someone. I would say that is a good day."

Asa shot a kiss at me. "Merry Christmas, Mother."

"Merry Christmas, Daughter."

45

It was a sunny morning and I was reading the newspaper by the back windows where the light was best.

There was the curious story on the front page about a young guest of Lady Elsmere's who opened her gun collection without permission and accidentally shot himself with an antique women's derringer on Christmas Day. It also stated that Lady Elsmere's nephew, Sir Anthony, would be returning to London after the holidays.

So that old bird covered everything up. I had to laugh and was still chuckling when the phone rang.

"Mrs. Reynolds?"

"This is she."

"This is Charlotte. Remember me? The lab technician."

I straightened up in my chair. "Yes, I do, Charlotte."

"I've finished the lab report. In fact, I did it twice just to be sure."

"Just put it in the mail, dear."

"I think you'd better come and get it personally. I wouldn't want it to get lost."

There was silence on my end as I tried to process what she was saying to me. "Okay. Can I pick it up tomorrow?"

"Yes, ma'am. Anytime between noon and five. I want to explain some things to you."

"I'll be there at one thirty."

"That's fine." She hung up.

What did she find that she couldn't tell me on the phone?

I didn't like the sound of it.

46

Charlotte showed me into the conference room. She had a sealed container with the chocolate horse and a lengthy report. She turned the file toward me. There were many areas highlighted with a yellow marker. She pointed to these areas with her pencil.

"The report conclusively states that the hairs from the horse were the same as the DNA in the hair sample that you supplied."

"You're positive?"

"It's 99.97 percent correct." Charlotte hesitated for a moment. "I did something I wasn't suppose to do, but you said this hunk of chocolate might solve the mystery of that missing man."

I nodded, waiting for her to continue.

"My boyfriend is studying to be a forensic anthropologist. His mentor is an expert in forensic osteology."

"What's that?"

"The study of the cause of death from bone fragments."

"But there are no bone fragments."

"Yes, there were . . . are. I found very tiny fragments stuck in the part of the horse where it looked like the leg had been melted and stuck back on."

"And?" I was finding it hard to breathe.

"They are part of a human tooth."

"Oh dear," was all I could say.

"The tooth fragments are too small to do anything other than to identify them as an adult human. Here's the report from my boyfriend's mentor, but he won't sign it as it is not official." Charlotte placed it in front of me. "I hope you're not angry with me."

I quickly read the sparse report. "No, no. Not at all. Just stunned. I was so hoping that the results would be different."

"This is about murder now, isn't it?"

"It could be any number of things, but it doesn't look good." I gathered up the report.

Charlotte put the container on a cart and wheeled it out to my car. She helped me put it in the back seat. "I could get into a lot of trouble for taking the tooth sample out of the lab."

"I'll keep your name out of this if I can but if something should arise, the police might want to talk with you," I replied.

"Let me know what happens."

"You bet." We shook hands and parted.

The problem was what do I do now?

47

I dumped the lab container on Goetz's desk.

"And a Happy New Year to you too," declared Goetz.

I placed a large hamper by his feet.

He kicked it under his desk and looked around to see if anyone had noticed.

"Two Cornish hens with wild rice and pecan stuffing, wilted swiss chard, old fashioned lettuce wedge with homemade blue cheese and bacon dressing, and an Apple Betty for dessert."

"Isn't an Apple Betty a little humble to go with Cornish hens?"

"It's what I had in the house."

"What can I do you for?"

"For you to do your job."

"I told you that a body was needed for further investigation."

I pulled out the bag with the tooth fragments from the container and threw it at him. "You got it."

Goetz picked up the bag, studying it.

"If you want the provenance of this chocolate, call up Ginny Wheelwright. I presume you have her number?"

"Do me a favor. Don't call me. I'll call you."

I started to leave. "Oh, Goetz."

"Yeah?"

"Happy New Year."

48

Asa had flown back to London, while Boris stayed a few more days to keep an eye on Farley.

He rolled in around eight one morning. I got up to fix him breakfast before he went to bed.

"Just some milk and pastry, please," requested Boris in his thick European accent. "No eggs or meat. Too heavy before I sleep."

I poured some hot tea in a clear glass, poured another glass with milk and retrieved some Danish out of the freezer, which I quickly nuked. Putting the food on a tray, I took it to the dining room table where Boris was already nodding off.

"Just resting my eyes," he muttered, jerking up in his seat.

I placed the food before him.

Boris smiled when he saw the glass of hot tea. "That is how we serve hot tea in my country. No fancy little cups."

"I know."

Boris hungrily tore at the pastry.

I waited until he had eaten.

Finishing his milk, he leaned back in the chair and closed his eyes again.

"Before you fall asleep, did you find out anything?"

Boris gave me a slippery smile. "Ya. Find out some things. Farley? He spends the night at his best friend Dwight's house. Left at six."

"That's juicy. But he and Selena could have hooked up after Dwight's disappearance. Doesn't mean anything."

"I think it does. He peeked through front curtains, seeing if anyone was outside. Then he looks around coming out. He is pretending . . . no, the word is sneaking. Don't want anyone to know he's there."

Boris pulled out a small digital camera and showed me the pictures.

It did indeed look like Farley was trying to leave the house undetected. But it still didn't prove anything.

"And this." Boris pulled a folded piece of paper from his pocket. He handed it to me.

"That Susie Brinkman, who said she lives in Houston now. Checked it out. No Susie Brinkman from Kentucky lives in Houston.

"I did more checking. There is a Susie Brinkman who lives in Waddy, Kentucky and works at insurance company in Frankfort. Here's address. I don't know if same Susie Brinkman but description matches." Boris yawned. "I go to bed now. When I wake up, you take me to airport. I fly to London."

I absent-mindedly nodded to Boris while looking at the information about Susie. Did that little button of a girl lie to me?

Tonight I would drive Boris to the Bluegrass Airport.

Tomorrow I would seek out one Susie Brinkman of Waddy, Kentucky.

49

I called Amanda early the next morning.

"Amanda, this is Josiah Reynolds."

"Hi."

"Just wanted to thank you again for giving me Susie's phone number."

"Did you get a hold of her?"

"Yeah. It was the strangest coincidence. When I got in touch, she just happened to be at the Bluegrass Airport waiting for a connection."

"What luck."

"Funny huh?"

"Yeah."

"Amanda, I just have a few more questions if you don't mind. What did Susie do at the office?"

"She handled all the paperwork for the office like the contracts."

"Did she handle insurance?"

"That's what she was best at. Susie had a real knack of understanding insurance of all types."

"Did she handle insurance for any of the employees in the office?"

"Of course. I went through Susie to get several policies and she handled all the health insurance policies."

"She handled life insurance?"

"Yes."

"You know that five hundred thousand dollar life insurance policy Dwight took out? Was that customary?"

"Most of us had smaller policies. Even Farley. I thought it odd that it would be so large an amount. I mean, Dwight was in excellent health and young. I didn't think he needed a big policy like that. The premiums would have been very high."

"Who handled that policy?"

"Susie."

"Thanks Amanda. That's all I wanted to know."

50

I waited in the parking lot of the address in Frankfort that Boris had given me. I figured Susie would be the type to eat lunch out. So I hunkered down looking through my binoculars, munching on my tuna fish sandwich.

Around 1:20, Susie rushed to her car in the parking lot. It was snowing, so she had her coat lapel pulled up around her face. Susie slowly drove out of the parking lot as it was covered with lots of black ice.

I followed at a discreet distance. Passing as she pulled into a chain restaurant's parking lot, I doubled back and parked in the handicapped space, which gave me a good view of her table. I waited for her to get settled and to make sure she wasn't having lunch with a friend.

After she placed her order, I got out of the car and headed inside. I made straight for her table.

"Hi," I chirped sprightly. "How ya doing, Susie?"

Susie gave a start.

"I'm so sorry. I didn't mean to startle you. I'm Mrs. Reynolds. Remember—we talked at the Bluegrass Airport. You were on your way to Houston."

Catching her breath, Susie decided to brave my sucker punch. "Yes, I remember. Do you have any news of Dwight?"

"He's still missing," I stated after telling the waitress I didn't want anything.

Susie looked downfallen. "Oh, that's terrible."

"Yeah, isn't it? Funny running into you like this. I still have some questions."

I could tell Susie was trying to figure out if I had followed her or this was really a chance meeting. She decided to play along.

"Anything I can do to help."

"Wonderful. Amanda said that you handled most of the office paperwork concerning insurance and health policies."

"That's correct."

"Did you help Dwight with his five-hundred-thousand dollar life insurance policy?"

"Yes."

"Amanda told me that no one else had such a large life insurance policy. Do you know why he took out such a large sum?"

"He wanted to make sure if something happened to him that Selena would never have to work."

"Then why was Selena's name not on the policy?"

Susie opened her mouth and closed it again. She truly looked stymied. "I don't know. Her name was on the policy as the only beneficiary when I did the paperwork. Dwight must have had it changed after I left."

"Why would he do that?"

Susie looked about for an escape. I could tell she was confused and just wanted to leave.

I lifted my cane on her booth seat so she would either have to push it out of the way or climb over it. Either way it would cause attention.

"Susie?"

"You're embarrassing me."

"It could get a lot worse. I'm notorious for causing scenes in public. Answer my questions truthfully and I will leave. But if I think you're lying, I will do something unexpected and the police will probably be called."

"Good," she hissed.

"I don't think so for you. I will call Detective Goetz and he will call the Frankfort police to hold you. The police will just give me a warning and let me go after I give them some lame story of my medication making me erratic. But they will make you wait for the indomitable Detective Goetz, who will want to know about your affair with Dwight Wheelwright and if you were really in Houston when he disappeared on July third."

"Go to hell," Susie ranted.

"I wouldn't make a run for it either. I let the air out of two of your tires before coming in." I grimaced. "Sorry about that."

"What do you want, bitch?"

"I can see that we are getting personal. Okay, you little twerp. Let's have some answers. Whose idea was it for the life insurance policy? Why would Dwight bother if he was going to leave anyway?"

"It was Selena. She had been after him for months about it. He wanted to get her off his back."

"Did she say why?"

"Just wanted that safety net, I guess. Dwight never discussed it with me. Just told me to get it."

"And she was the only beneficiary?"

"Yes. I know that for a fact."

"So it is a surprise to you that her name is not on the policy now?"

Susie nodded before taking a sip of water. She dabbed a paper napkin in the water glass and patted her face.

"Were you really having an affair with Dwight?"

Susie paused for a moment and then said, "Yes."

"Susie. You know, if Dwight's body pops up and his cause of death is murder, you might be charged with being an accessory or interfering with an investigation. I can think of several charges that might apply."

Susie's eyes took on the look that a rabbit has when she sees a big bobcat getting ready to pounce. "All right. I didn't have an affair with Dwight."

"Who told you to say that you did?"

"Farley. Farley paid me to tell anyone who asked to say that Dwight and I had been having an affair."

"You didn't think that bizarre?"

"Yes, I thought it strange but the money was too good. I took it and didn't ask any questions."

I gave Susie an odd look.

"Don't you dare judge me," spat out Susie. "I needed the money. I had some serious bills."

"Did Farley give a reason why?" I asked.

"Just some bullshit excuse that Dwight wanted out and he was asking too much money for his half, so Farley wanted to stir up a little trouble for Dwight. Make his life a little miserable with Selena so Dwight would want out quicker and with less money."

"I don't see how that works."

"Uh, duh, Selena thinks I'm having an affair with Dwight and pressures him to make a deal with Farley so Dwight would leave the business fast. He wouldn't see me then."

"Uh, duh, Susie, let's say that's true. How was that going to keep you two apart? Dwight could have seen you whenever he wanted. He didn't have to go to the office to have an affair."

"Not if Selena put the kibosh on him. If Dwight denied having an affair with me, then she would think he was lying and keep him on a shorter leash."

"Let me get this straight. Farley tells you that Dwight wants out and is negotiating for more money than Farley wanted to pay."

Susie nodded her head.

"So Farley gets this idea that if he makes life miserable for Dwight by telling Selena that he is having an affair with a woman in the office, Selena will put pressure on Dwight to settle," I repeated.

"That was the plan."

"Did you ever talk to Selena?"

"Never saw her."

"Did Dwight ever confront you?" I asked.

"No. He was cordial."

"Why did you leave?"

"Farley thought it best before things exploded in the office. That's what he said anyway. He got me this job in Frankfort with a buddy of his. It's closer to home so I save money on gas. I'm happy with it plus I have the money Farley paid me." Susie gave me a pained expression. I think it had just dawned on her how stupid she had been.

"So the only person you discussed this plan with was Farley?"

"And you. You were the only person who ever asked about it. Supposedly Farley told Selena this story and I was to back him up if she confronted me about it," Susie confessed.

"Did Farley call you and tell you to expect my call?"

"Yeah. He told me he would pay me more money if I were to act as though I had been living in Houston and had been waiting for Dwight. I was at work when you called and probably got to the airport just minutes before you did."

"That was a pretty good play–seeing me at the airport."

"I thought it was rather smart. I knew when those Houston flights came in. If the flight had been a later time, I would have told you that I was still in Houston waiting for a flight and given you a later time to meet me at the airport. It was easy."

"I wondered why you didn't have any luggage with you," I remarked.

Susie flashed me a smile. She thought I was complimenting her cleverness.

"I didn't know Dwight was missing until Farley told me. I don't take the paper or listen to the news. Too much stress. I was shocked," admitted Susie. "After seeing you, I thought about calling Dwight's mother, but I realized I was in too deep. Something was not right and I didn't want to get into trouble. Nobody from Dwight's office really knew where I was currently living so I thought I was safe."

"Did you ever go to Houston?"

"My mother remarried and moved there a few years ago. I did visit several weeks before I started my new job in Frankfort. As far as I was concerned, I had just helped one of my bosses screw the other in a buyout. It was business. Nothing more. But Dwight's disappearance is something else. I didn't bargain on that."

"Do you think Farley had anything to do with Dwight's disappearance?"

"Heavens no," laughed Susie. "Farley's a schemer, but that's about it. He was just trying to knock the price down. If you want to look at someone, size up Selena. Now there's a piece of work."

"Why do you say that?"

"It's what I inferred from all the stories Farley told me about her. He doesn't like her. Said she was holding Dwight back. Always nagging."

I didn't know whom to believe. Everyone was telling the wildest stories and they did all seem to lead to Farley. If Farley disliked Selena so much, what was he doing sneaking out of her house at six in the morning?

"I want you to do something for me and I'm not going to pay you," I demanded.

"Oh yeah?"

"Yeah. I want you to contact the insurance company that issued Dwight's life insurance policy and find out who instigated the changing of the beneficiaries and anything else you can dig out from them."

"What's in it for me?" Susie insisted.

"You've got to be kidding."

"I can give you the answer right now. Only Dwight could change the beneficiary."

"Just find out. Maybe someone other than Dwight made the call. I want to see who."

Susie sighed while slumping her shoulders in defeat. "I guess I could do that."

I just wanted to slap her stupid little face so much my hand twitched. "You have my number." I got up to leave.

"If I were Dwight and had this on my plate, I would have just run off. Dwight's probably in Florida right now having a good time, while the rest of us are worried sick."

"Well, you're not Dwight. He's not a runner. He's missing because something happened to him."

Susie sneered at me. "And I guess you think you're going to be the big honcho to solve his disappearance. Lady, you're old and can barely walk. You're good for nothing except being a nuisance."

I gave Susie my sweetest smile. "In addition to letting the air out of your tires, I broke your side mirror. It was an accident. I stumbled into it since I can't walk–just like you said. Bye, bye now."

On the way out I heard Susie rush behind me and squawk about the damage to her car. As I was leaving the parking lot, she was on her cell phone–no doubt to the police about my vandalism.

I didn't care. I really didn't care.

She had hurt my friends with her lies and she was lying now. I just couldn't pluck out the truth from the lies, but I would.

God as my witness, I surely would.

51

I confessed everything to Detective Goetz.

He leaned back in his chair and peered over his new glasses. "That was very unladylike of you. I'm surprised."

"Haven't you heard a word I've said?"

"How do you know this Susie Brinkman didn't make advances toward Wheelwright and was rejected? Maybe she's making stuff up for revenge?" asked Goetz.

"She called later after talking to the insurance company and an acquaintance in the office told her that Dwight came in himself and changed the name of the beneficiaries, giving the excuse that Selena was to receive a large bequest from her parents. My question is—was she?"

"No. I've already checked their finances. They don't have any money or at least I couldn't find a record of it."

"Doesn't this whole thing about the life insurance policy strike you as odd?" I asked.

"Maybe," Goetz replied, shuffling some papers on his desk.

"What about the tooth?"

"You want to go out with me sometime?" Goetz asked suddenly.

I reared back in my chair. "I thought you didn't like me."

"I can tolerate you in small doses."

"Wow. What a compliment. Let's get back to talking about the case."

"If that's the way you want it."

"The tooth fragments," I insisted.

"His mother had kept all of Dwight's baby teeth, so we did a DNA test after a cast was made of the tooth fragments. It turned out as you suspected. The tooth fragments were Dwight's. It's enough for a warrant in my book, even though the DA has some serious problems with the chain of evidence."

"So you are finally taking this seriously."

"There wasn't a time I didn't take his disappearance seriously. You seem to forget that I am a homicide detective. I needed justifiable cause to proceed."

"Which I provided. What—no thank you?" I retorted.

"Since we are on that subject, you are to butt out. No more inquiries. If I hear that you are still snooping around, I will arrest you for interfering with an official investigation. I mean it."

I started to interrupt him, but I could tell from his demeanor that he meant what he said. "Will you keep me informed?"

"Hell no."

"If that's the way you want to leave it." I gathered my cane and rose from the old-fashioned wooden swivel chair.

Goetz walked me out. "You wouldn't be sorry going out with me."

"Oh, that again. If you're such a catch, how come your wife divorced you and your girlfriend moved to Florida?"

"They said I was married to the police force."

"Aren't you supposed to retire soon?"

"Yep, but then I'm going to work in the District Attorney's office."

"Double-dipping."

"Goetz gave me a big smile.

I had forgotten that he had dimples when he genuinely smiled. Thinking back, I realized when I had last seen him smile like that. It was on the first day we met, when he and O'nan had interrogated me about Richard Pidgeon's demise.

Anger bubbled up my throat just remembering that day.

"I gotta go," I said suddenly, and rushed out of the police station.

It wasn't until I reached my car that I realized I was crying.

52

There was a knock on the door. Baby ran to the front door, panting excitedly and wagging his tail. I knew it was someone he was familiar with but still I checked the monitors.

It was Ginny Wheelwright!

I opened the door.

"Ginny!"

"May I come in, Jo?"

"Yes. Of course."

Eunice came for Baby.

"Let's go in my office. We won't be bothered there."

As we were going down the hall, I heard Eunice telling Baby to go outside and play. Then I heard the door slam. Eunice was one human Baby didn't cross. She believed in swatting a bad dog. It only took one swat of a newspaper on Baby's fanny for him to get the idea that Eunice was the alpha. He minded her without question. Wish I could say the same.

I closed the office door while Ginny sat down.

"What's up?" I asked.

"Detective Goetz has re-opened the case, but with few results so far. He got warrants to search Selena's house and Dwight's office. Amanda and that Susie Brinkman have given official statements."

Ginny sniffed.

I handed her a tissue. It was confounding that Ginny never had anything to wipe her nose. "Keep the box," I insisted.

Ginny nodded thanks as she pulled out a wad of tissues. "Detective Goetz has been wonderful. He even tracked down that lead on a scorpion bite."

"And?"

"Nothing incriminating was found at Selena's house, although the Detective did find a record of a cashier's check made out to Dwight for two hundred thousand dollars. But the law firm working for Dwight's company said they were never approached to write a buyout agreement for Dwight. It was the first that they had heard of it, but they did confirm what Farley had told you about what would happen if one partner was incapacitated."

"Where's that money now?"

"The check was never cashed. Selena doesn't have it. Goetz checked."

"Did Selena opt to sell her portion?"

"She decided to remain as a silent partner. Farley pays her a dividend every quarter, but she has no say in the business."

"What about Susie's story of Farley paying her?"

"Farley denied it, of course. Said she was trying to get him into trouble, as he had fired her. It's an issue of he said/she said."

"Isn't there a money trail?"

"Goetz couldn't find any evidence that Farley paid her because Susie said she had been paid in cash. There's just no way to tie the cash to Farley."

I sat back in my chair and looked out the window. I didn't want to talk about this anymore. I was sick of the case. It depressed me.

Ginny continued, "I know if it hadn't been for you that none of this information would have been discovered. I still don't know what happened to Dwight, but I realize that the investigation went further than anticipated due to your efforts. I never could have done it. I wouldn't have even known where to start. My only idea to help was to put up posters." She opened her purse and laid a check on the desk. "This should cover all the lab expenses and your gas money. It took me a while to raise the money, but here it is."

I remained silent. What was there to say anyway?

Ginny rose from her chair. "As long as I live, I will never forget what you did for me."

I still didn't say anything.

"I'll see myself out." She quietly closed the door to the office.

I sat for a long time looking out the window. The ground was thick with snow while tree limbs drooped from the snow's weight.

Any hope that Dwight was still alive had faded to a shadow. The check was to be his ticket to freedom and it had not been cashed. If he were still alive, he certainly would have cashed it.

The thought that Dwight was buried in some unmarked grave made me ill. I was tired of seeing lives ruined. Dwight's. My daughter's.

No one passes through this life unscathed.

Baby scratched at the closed office door.

I reluctantly got up and opened it. I was in no mood to put up with his chicanery.

Baby butted me with his head. He wanted his ears scratched. I reached down and pulled on his silky ears and gently rubbed the scar caused by O'nan's bullet. I touched his eyeless socket.

Baby's tail wagged enthusiastically.

His joy at being petted made me feel better. If Baby could be happy after being shot three times, who was I to wallow in sadness.

"Eunice, I'm coming," I called as I rushed to help her.

53

The winter had been long and hard.

In the middle of February, we had an ice storm that shut the city down for a week. No one had electricity except the hospitals and a few government buildings. Cracked and broken trees were blocking the main arteries and side roads as well. Schools, including the University of Kentucky, cancelled classes. No one ventured out unless they had four-wheel drive as the roads were covered with ice.

All was quiet. Much of daily life had ground to a halt.

Regretting that he had ignored my advice about installing a wood stove in his newly renovated house, Matt took refuge at the Butterfly.

Not too long after that Franklin followed, as his apartment was an icebox.

Franklin was followed by Lady Elsmere, who was deposited on my doorstep by Charles.

"What are you going to do, Charles?" I asked. "I can't believe your generators are on the blink too."

"My family is going to stay at one of the barns. I've already had wood delivered, so we'll be fine. I'll check on June every day. Call me if she needs anything," he said.

"Will you be at Barn Number Two?" That was the barn that had an apartment with a wood stove, kitchen and two bedrooms. Everything in the kitchen ran on propane, including the refrigerator.

"Yeah, we'll be hunkered down there. The boys have gone to stay with their friends, so it will just be the missus and the girls," replied Charles.

"Let's keep in touch a couple times of day," I advised.

"Sounds good," agreed Charles. "I'll be back today, so call if you need anything." Waving, he started the Hummer down the driveway.

Passing him on the way was Matt returning from the barn after checking on the animals. The animals had to be checked several times a day. Their water would freeze, so someone had to break the thick layer of ice so they could drink.

I held the door open for him.

Matt carried a large box into the house, which he deposited quickly in front of the fireplace. "Hey Baby, your buddies are here."

I stood back and watched as confused and anxious cats sprang out of the box and ran for the nearest nook in which to hide.

"I couldn't leave them in the barn. They were freaking out."

"How about the rest of my babies?"

"Seem to be doing fine. I started the generator so that should give them some heat since it will be well below zero tonight. Put plenty of straw and hay in everyone's stalls."

"Did you put the goats in with the horses?"

"Naw. I put them with the sheep. They're getting along."

"What about the baby llama?"

"She and her mama are okay. I fed everyone. Don't worry. They're fine." Matt patted my shoulder. "I'll check on them again before dark."

"Did you put food out for the deer?"

Exasperated, Matt declared, "I put out food, water, and a salt lick. And I filled all the bird feeders. All God's creatures are fine."

"Where're you going now?"

"I'm going to take a nap. Is that okay with you?"

I gave Matt a sassy grin. "Quit being so irritable. I'll fix you something to eat."

Matt harrumphed as he turned. He was getting crabbier as he got older.

"Hey, Matt."

"What!!!"

"Thanks for being here."

Matt shook his head. "Where else would I be?"

I was going into the kitchen to fix "Mr. Grumpy" some grub when the phone rang.

It was Ginny. "Jo, I need to ask a favor. Can you drive me over to Selena's? She's got electricity. I know it's an imposition, but I've called everyone including the cab company and volunteer drivers. They are overwhelmed and can't get to me until tonight. I'm freezing over here and you have access to 4-wheel drive. Jo. Jo? Are you there?"

"Let me see if Matt can get you. He's got the only car that can make it. Hold on."

I went to Matt's room and peeked in. Matt was on the bed sound asleep. No way was I going to wake him for Ginny. But I didn't want to go out in this weather.

I thought of calling Charles but he would be busy tending the horses in the barns all day, so he was out. I went back to the phone. "Ginny, I'll get there as soon as I can."

"Okay, but hurry. I don't even have water."

I hung up and went to find my boots. Buttoned up in a big flannel coat, I grabbed Matt's keys and told Franklin where I was going.

"Can't she wait for a cab?"

"She's older than I and has health problems."

"And you don't?"

"Selena doesn't have 4-wheel. I'm going. Should be back before dark. Keep June happy, will you."

"I don't think this is a good idea."

"Oh, Franklin, keep the wood stove going, will you."

"Sure thing. Matt's gonna be mad."

"Hopefully, I'll be back before he wakes up."

I pulled open the front door and braved the cold, hurrying to Matt's new SUV.

Going down Tates Creek was a nightmare. Everywhere were tree limbs that had snapped off due to the weight of the ice. I came to a downed tree and power lines that blocked the road. Backing up, I retraced my steps back to the little village of Spears. I drove down Spears Road toward Richmond Road.

All during the drive, I heard cracks and groans as the trees shifted, trying to shrug off their burden of ice. I made it to Richmond Road, which was a main artery into town. Thank goodness the road had been plowed and salted. Now making good time, I reached Ginny's house.

Having stood watch at her picture window, Ginny saw me pull in her driveway and came out in a hurry with an overnight bag and her cat, Puss Puss.

"Jo, I so appreciate this. Really, I do."

"Let's hurry. I've got to get back to the farm."

It took me another twenty minutes to drive to Selena's house as most of the traffic lights were out and all the side roads had not been cleared. I sighed with relief when I pulled into her cleared driveway.

"You coming in?"

"Yeah. I need to use the restroom and I wouldn't mind a cup of hot tea before I head out again," I requested, grabbing the cat carrier while Ginny got her overnight bag. We trudged over the crunchy ice into Selena's house.

"What took you so long?" exclaimed Selena, looking put out. "We had lunch hours ago."

Putting Puss Puss' carrier down, I pulled off my gloves. "The roads were bad and all the traffic lights were on the blink. And I had to come from the farm." *What an idiot!* I thought.

"But it's only ten miles from Man O' War to your place."

"Selena, what can I tell you. It has taken me an hour and a half to get your mother-in-law here. I am going to use your bathroom now. I would really appreciate a cup of hot tea before I head out."

I didn't give her time to say anything as I made way to the bathroom. I tinkled, washed my hands, and put on fresh lipstick. I took a hit of albuterol spray, as the cold air was not good for my asthma. That should have been enough time for Selena to have a cup of hot liquid on the table.

When I came into the kitchen, Ginny was scurrying around Selena. She put a mug of steaming hot tea in front of me along with a nice hunk of coffee cake. "Thanks again for getting me. I really appreciate it. Wasn't that nice of Josiah, Selena?"

"Yeah, it was nice," mumbled Selena before she drifted off into another room.

I whispered, "You sure you don't want to come back with me to the Butterfly?"

Ginny shook her head. "I want to be with my grandchild. The storm gives me an excuse to see her."

"Okay. But I'm not coming out again, Ginny. You'll have to stick it out if things go south."

"Drink your tea, Josiah. It's getting cold."

She didn't have to tell me twice. I dove into the coffee cake and sipped my tea. The stack of vacation pictures was still on the kitchen table. I pulled out a bunch and began to peruse them. Just something to do while sipping my tea. There were quite a few of Selena and Dwight at the beach, looking very young and happy.

Ginny joined me. I handed her a stack of pictures after I had looked at them. Apparently Selena and Dwight had taken lots of vacations over their ten years of marriage. It was nice to see them beaming for the camera. Then I came across a few with Dwight, Selena, and Farley. These pictures seemed more worn and bent at the corners . . . as if they had been handled more often. They were at Devou Park in Covington. There were quite a few pictures of the three of them standing transposed with the skyline of Cincinnati behind them. Obviously they had had a stranger take pictures of the three of them.

Then one caught my attention. It was a close-up of Selena facing the camera with Dwight in the background with his back turned looking at the skyline of Cincinnati. I realized that Farley must have taken this picture. What struck me was the expression of Selena looking straight into the camera. But she wasn't looking at the camera.

She was looking at the person taking the picture and it was the look of love.

I slid the picture into my coat pocket when Ginny went to refill her mug. "Ginny, do you know when these pictures were taken? That's Devou Park. I used to sled down this hill they're standing on."

"Great view, isn't it. I think those were taken several years ago." Ginny thought for a moment. "Yes, it was two years ago. Dwight and Farley were attending a conference in Cincinnati and Selena decided to go with them. I took care of the baby."

There was no point in pursuing this with Ginny. She was trapped with Selena until her power came back on.

I said my goodbyes and headed out to Matt's cold car. I had a time getting the door open, as it had frozen shut. The next-door neighbor, who was out shoveling snow, helped me pry it open.

Thank goodness for the kindness of strangers.

Heading back to the house, it began to snow heavily. I made better time as the snow gave the SUV better traction than the ice and I was able to make it home in an hour. That gave me plenty of time to "bend my mind around that picture," as the locals would say.

Goetz was wrong about one thing.

It was becoming clearer to me that Dwight had met an awful fate, but it wasn't from the hands of strangers. It might have come at him from those he had loved and trusted.

Ain't love grand!

54

"You're to stay in the car."

"But you might not ask the right questions," I whined.

"I've been asking the right questions for close to three decades. I think I know what I'm doing," retorted Goetz.

"But it's my theory."

"That's the only reason you're along for the ride. I have my doubts. You can't kill someone with a piece of chocolate, no matter how damn big the piece is."

"I think you can. In fact, I ordered a centerpiece exactly like the one Ginny did. I'm going to give it to Charlotte's boyfriend to do an experiment since your lab is too cheap to do so. In fact," I said, getting out of the car, "I ordered it from here."

I went inside the candy shop, ignoring Goetz's hateful looks.

Kentucky is known for certain types of food: country ham and beaten biscuits, mint juleps, burgoo, fried chicken, Kentucky Hot Brown, Kentucky Bourbon and Pecan cake, Derby Pie, but nothing says Kentucky like Bourbon balls.

A Bourbon ball is a bite-size candy made with chocolate, powdered sugar, pecans, and lots and lots of bourbon. A pecan half traditionally sits on top of the candy.

Ruth Booe, known as Mrs. Boo, invented Bourbon balls, after a dignitary, Eleanor Hume Offutt, suggested mixing Kentucky Bourbon with chocolate in 1936. Thus a great candy was born.

I tell you this so you will understand why I bought six boxes of Bourbon balls along with my chocolate centerpiece. I love them and Lady Elsmere expects them when she comes "a calling." Just a little tidbit of information.

The clerk called into the candy-making room for John. We could see John through the glass that separated the candy room from the sales room. He went into a freezer and brought out a huge box. Inside was my chocolate horse.

"Is this the exact model that Ginny Wheelwright bought last year?"

"Terrible about her son, isn't it."

I nodded.

"This is the same mold we used for Miss Ginny's horse. She had ordered it a month before. We usually don't do horse centerpieces unless it's around Derby time and then we do a lot for private parties and hotels. That sort of thing. We're known for this chocolate horse."

"What's the weight on this thing?" asked Goetz.

John scratched his chin. "It comes in a little under twenty-three pounds. It's solid chocolate."

"Why's it frozen?" I asked. "It has a bloom on it. The chocolate is discolored."

"The horse is always kept either in a cooler or a freezer until several hours before use. It's to keep the chocolate firm. As you can see, the legs are like the legs of a real Thoroughbred. They need to stay firm to support the rest of the centerpiece. Now we have an arm connecting the horse to its platform, which helps to support the centerpiece, but sometimes the horse will still tip over. We have to be careful with them."

"But it looks ugly with the discoloration."

"That's nothing. Right before it is placed on the table, a hair dryer is used to take off the bloom. Makes the chocolate shiny. The instructions come with the horse."

"Wouldn't freezing it make the chocolate brittle?"

"Especially the delicate parts. That's why we recommend that it stay in its container until several hours before it is presented or it's at a cool room temperature. Don't take it out hours before and put it on a table on a hot day . . . say if the event is taking place in a tent or something like that. One just has to use common sense when gauging the temperature."

"I take it that if the centerpiece falls or is dropped . . ." pointed out Goetz.

John interrupted. "Then parts of the horse might shatter like the neck or the legs if cold. The main body will be okay. Usually it's the horse's mane or tail that gets mangled first. That's why it should stay in its container upright until right before presentation."

"If a leg snaps off, can it be put back on?"

"Sure thing. Just use the hair dryer to heat the break and seal it back together again. That happens to us and we just stick the legs back on. When we're done, you can't even tell."

"I guess an amateur couldn't make it look as nice as you."

John shrugged. "It depends on the person's skill."

"Did Ginny Wheelwright pick up her horse in person?"

"Yes," interrupted the sales woman. "I waited on her personally. It was on the thirtieth of June. She was very happy with the horse. She buys a large chocolate piece every year for her son. I mean she used to buy."

"Was the horse in good condition?"

The sales lady in her pink apron pulled out a receipt from a drawer. "I got this out of our files when you called." She handed it to Goetz. "The horse was perfect." She pointed to writing on the receipt. "See, I even wrote down what Miss Ginny said about it. She said it was the best one she had gotten for her son. She was very pleased with it."

"The reason we sell so many of these large centerpieces is that the horse looks like it's in motion."

"Yes. It's lovely," I concurred.

"Thank you for your time," nodded Goetz as he picked up the box.

I picked up my Bourbon balls, thanked John and his clerk before following Goetz out to his car. He put the horse into the trunk.

"What now?" I asked.

"I guess we go see if we can kill a man with a chocolate horse."

55

Goetz and I went to the lab following closing hours. It wasn't long after I knocked on the glass door that Charlotte let us.

"Thank you for doing this, Charlotte," I said.

"Has everything been set up?" asked Goetz, looking into offices as we passed.

"Sure. We've got a camera recording the experiment and can give you a copy before you leave."

"I'll want the media card," advised Goetz.

"But Dr. Cardello wants a copy to show his students."

"No can do at this time. It's part of an investigation. Maybe afterwards."

Charlotte looked miffed. "Well, you tell him. My boyfriend and Dr. Cardello went to a lot of trouble and expense."

"Send me a bill and I will have the city reimburse them." Goetz handed Charlotte his business card.

She looked at it before putting it in her pocket. "If the city is going to reimburse us, then I guess it's okay."

We walked into a cavernous laboratory where two men were adjusting a pole upon which rested a replicate of a human head made out of some sort of pink shiny gel. A pair of dentures was inserted where the mouth would be on a human.

The men turned when they heard us enter the room.

Charlotte whispered in Dr. Cardello's ear. She must have told him about not keeping a copy, as he didn't look pleased. But he didn't mention it as he greeted us, shaking our hands after Goetz set down the box with the horse.

"Let me show you what I've done," prompted Dr. Cardello.

I could tell Dr. Cardello liked being the center of attention. He must have loved the attention of having Charlotte and her boyfriend look admiringly at him.

"This pole is flexible and I can tighten to what I think proper in any given experiment. I have given it the same flexibility that I think a man weighing 172 pounds and the height of 5 feet, 10 inches would have if hit in the face. He would swing back or fall down completely. I've made it so that an impact would make his body sway like this." Dr. Cardello gave a brief demonstration.

"The head is made from a special plastic that acts as skin." He knocked on it. "It looks wet, but is not. It is dry and feels like the real thing." He pushed on the cheek. It made an indentation that rebounded like actual skin would. "Underneath is Styrofoam shaped like an adult skull."

"We thought about using a watermelon, but decided this would be better," teased Charlotte.

Both Dr. Cardello and the boyfriend beamed at Charlotte.

I had a brief uncomfortable thought that maybe Charlotte was doing both of them. Hope the boyfriend didn't find out.

Dr. Cardello clapped his hands together. "Let's see the weapon of choice."

Goetz pulled the chocolate horse out of its container and put it on the table.

Charlotte, the boyfriend, and Dr. Cardello circled the horse, giving it their rapt attention.

"Do we know at what temperature the horse was when used?" asked Dr. Cardello.

"We are assuming it was frozen or near frozen," I replied.

Goetz leaned forward and pointed to the front left leg. "This part would have made contact with the mouth. That's where the tooth fragments were found. Right, Charlotte?"

"Yes, right there," pointed Charlotte.

"That would indicate that the attacker was right-handed," advised Dr. Cardello.

"Does anyone know how it was displayed?"

"I do," I piped up. "It was turned this way and the break on the horse was here." I pointed to the horse's legs.

"Charlotte, you are the height and weight of the average woman. Let's stand you here. And Nathan, you are about the weight and height of the missing man. I am going to stand you in front of Charlotte, facing her. Yes. That's good." Dr. Cardello looked to Goetz for approval.

Goetz gave a little nod.

"Now—we don't know what tooth the fragments are from. Right?"

"That's correct," answered Goetz. "We don't have a body as of yet. And you stand by the conclusion that the fragments were from a tooth?"

"I'd swear in a court of law," replied Dr. Cardello.

"Okay. Charlotte. Pick up the horse and swing it at Nathan, but don't make contact. We just want to look at the motion at this point."

Charlotte reached over and tried to pick up the horse in one hand. Finding that she couldn't get her hand secure enough to lift it, she had to put both hands around the middle of the horse in order to lift it.

"Now swing it," admonished Dr. Cardello.

Charlotte gave it her best, almost dropping the horse in the process.

Goetz grabbed it before it fell. He grimaced at me. "That rules out Selena. She's smaller than this little gal."

"That depends," Dr. Cardello added. "If a woman was angry, she might have the adrenaline surge to swing it."

Shaking her head, Charlotte admitted, "It was too slippery. See, it's sweating now."

"What if the horse had been out of the box for a while and heated with a hair dryer?" asked Goetz.

"There were no handprints around the middle of the horse. Only the front left leg was mangled. I remember Ginny showing me the damage before the party. She was very upset."

"What about the platform it was on?"

"Just like this horse, it was on a thick corrugated platform sprinkled with a glittery powder or sugar. But I didn't see the platform, as Hershey kisses had been placed all around the horse and on the platform covering it. If it had been damaged, no one would have seen it. The platform was not in the garbage where the horse was found."

Dr. Cardello motioned to Nathan. "Let's see if you can pick up the horse and swing it."

Nathan changed places with Charlotte while Dr. Cardello placed the stick figure in front of him. "Now, Nathan, do what Charlotte did, but don't hit our dummy yet. I want to place a net to catch the horse just in case." Dr. Cardello put thick bubble wrap all around the stick dummy. "Okay. Try it."

Nathan's right hand easily grasped the horse and he swung it slowly toward the dummy.

All of us brightened at seeing this.

Nathan put the horse carefully back on the table.

"Now, Nathan, pick up the horse and swing it hard, as though you mean to strike a person. Be mad. Be really forceful," requested Dr. Cardello.

Nathan gave Charlotte one last glance before taking several deep breaths. Giving a terrible cry, Nathan picked up the horse and slammed it into the dummy's head.

The two front legs of the horse shattered, but much of the horse remained intact and in good condition. Nathan put the horse down and licked chocolate off his palm.

We all stepped forward to evaluate the head.

The left side of the face was crushed. Several teeth were missing.

The head looked as if it had been smashed with a hammer.

Goetz's expression didn't change. He just said, "Doc, I'll need several copies of that tape."

56

Even after Goetz showed the tooth fragments and the tape of the experiment to the DA, the case went nowhere.

The tooth fragments and the chocolate horse retrieved from Selena's garbage were dismissed as evidence, as the police had not properly bagged them into the chain of evidence.

The DA would not pursue the case further until there was a body, even though Goetz requested a warrant to dig up the yards of Selena and Farley. Nor would the DA go to a judge requesting a subpoena for Farley's or Selena's phone and bank records.

As Goetz was formulating a new theory of what had happened to Dwight, Selena and Farley had "lawyered-up" and refused to cooperate any further with the police. All contact had to go through their lawyers.

I even received a nicely worded letter from Selena's lawyer demanding that I quit being a pest and that legal action would ensue if I should have any future contact with her family or property.

This case was a mess. There seemed more questions than answers. There were just too many loose ends.

Where was the missing cashiers check for two hundred thousand dollars?

Why did Billy Klotter say he found Dwight's wallet in the rented fishing boat while the Whitley County police report said that it was found in the glove compartment of Dwight's pickup?

Then there were the two separate statements from the Dupont Lodge desk clerks, Darlene and Steve, contradicting each other identifying Dwight's picture.

And Goetz could never find a medical report of a scorpion bite concerning anyone involved in the case, though he tracked down all the emergency rooms and clinics near Laurel Lake.

It was another dead end.

As the days drifted into weeks and the weeks became months, even Ginny gave up hope that Dwight might still be alive somewhere.

Kentucky had a hard winter that year. Spring had to fight its way through the late snows and unusual cold temperatures to establish a foothold in the Bluegrass.

I went on with my life and didn't see Ginny again for some time. I left several messages for her to call, but she never did. I even went to her house once, and seeing that her car was gone, left a note on her front door, but she never contacted me.

That's how grief affects some people.

They act as though they're living, but they're really dead. Or they might as well be.

57

"So what do you think really happened to Dwight?" asked Matt over a cup of tea.

He and I were seated on the patio taking in the warm day.

Matt had taken the cover off the pool, and perhaps in a few days the swimming season could start. Especially if the days were sunny.

"Do you think the pool should be converted into a salt pool?" I replied, ignoring his question.

"Why are you being so hesitant?"

"Because I don't want to get sued."

"I'm your lawyer. Everything you say to me is confidential."

"Bull. You tell Franklin and then Franklin tells the world."

"Honest. I won't breathe a word."

"Speaking of Franklin, what's going on there?"

"Nothing."

"Then why is Franklin hanging around? He thinks he is going to help with the baby. Don't be cruel to him again, Matt. Cut Franklin loose if you are finished with him."

"That's exactly why nothing is going on. I made a big mess of things . . . with him and then with Meriah. When Meriah told me she was flying back to Los Angeles alone, I was relieved. Oh, I acted like it was a big crushing blow in order to save her feelings, but I felt like a condemned man who had gotten a stay of execution."

"Matt, you need to keep your pants zipped up until you decide which team you're gonna play on."

"I don't fall in love with a gender. I fall in love with a person. But you're right. I wasn't ready to commit to either Meriah or Franklin. I thought I was. I really did."

"You were being a jerk."

"Tell me how you really feel." Matt ran his hand through his dark curly hair. "Are you finished bashing me this morning? Can we discuss how you mangled evidence in Dwight's case and made it useless in a court of law? I wish you had talked to me before you took that chocolate to a private lab. I could have told you that a judge wouldn't admit it as evidence."

"I was a jerk too. A well meaning jerk, but a jerk just the same."

"Let me record you saying this, as no one will believe it."

I wrapped my blanket tighter around me. I could see my breath in the air when I talked. "I have several theories of what happened. Here's my favorite . . . is that the phone? Wait a minute. I'll be back."

*

I returned several minutes later after talking on the phone. "That was Ginny. It was just as Goetz predicted."

"What are you talking about?"

"Two hikers in the Daniel Boone Forest were going along one of the back trails and their dog found a lower mandible. It's human."

"And?"

"The police checked it with Dwight's dental records." I paused for a moment, trying to get my bearings. I looked out at the expanse of the Palisades where the wild dogwood trees were starting to bud. I took a deep breath. "It's Dwight."

Matt didn't respond. He just stared at the tea cooling in his mug. What was there to say anyway?

"They are searching for the rest of his remains now. It seems that animals have scattered the bones." I took a deep breath. "Ginny asked me to take her to Dupont Lodge. She wants to be there for the search."

"I would advise against that."

"You can't keep a mother away from her child . . . even her dead child. This is what mothers do."

"I have a few days off. I'll drive you and Ginny down there. You both are in no shape to drive yourselves. If I need to come back sooner, then I'll rent a car."

"Let me pack a bag."

Matt pulled out his cell phone. "I'll call Dupont Lodge and make reservations. You get ready."

"Thanks, Matt."

"And Rennie," said Matt using his pet name for me.

"Yeah."

"Make sure you pack your pain medication. Take some extra."

I gave Matt a strange look, but decided to do as he said. I'd rather have too much medication with me than not enough.

After letting Baby off at the Big House with Charles, we were on our way to pick up Ginny and then it was off to the Daniel Boone National Forest where the trees are so thick, sunlight barely shines on the ground.

It is a dark and foreboding place . . . truly a dark and bloody ground.

58

When we got to Dupont Lodge, I noticed Goetz's car in the parking lot. After we went to our respective rooms, I went to the dining room. I knew Goetz would have lunch first before he went to the field. That man never missed a meal.

"Christ," he uttered when I sat down. He threw his napkin on the table in disgust.

"That makes me feel like you're not happy to see me," I pouted.

"Anyone ever tell you that you're like a bad penny."

I turned to the waitress and told her that I would have the buffet. They were still serving breakfast and I wanted some pancakes . . . and bacon . . . maybe some biscuits with gravy . . . the eggs looked good . . . and grits.

"And this from the man who asked me out on a date."

"After thinking about it, I realized I'm too fat and too tired to do a woman any good."

"TMI. TMI!" I cried, making the sign of the cross.

"Quit acting like a schoolgirl," growled Goetz. "We both look like we were rode hard and put up wet."

"Oh, Detective Goetz! You're making me feel all tingly inside."

"I doubt I could make you feel tingly anywhere."

"Can we change the subject from my lady parts, please? Why are you here? You are out of your jurisdiction."

"I want to observe."

"Didn't you think he had been killed by a random thief?"

"That was before we found a tooth embedded in a chocolate horse."

"Fragments."

"It will be enough." He motioned for the waitress. "I take it Mrs. Wheelwright is here."

"She's in her room resting. She's already checked in with the State Police liaison, so they know she's here in case they find something."

Goetz shook his head. "A mother's love."

"The other Mrs. Wheelwright here?"

"There is no other Mrs. Wheelwright."

"What do you mean by that?"

Goetz smirked as he pulled out his wallet and left a tip on the table. "I finally know something that you don't. Wonders never cease." He put his wallet back in his coat pocket. "Mrs. Wheelwright is now Mrs. Webb."

"GET OUT! Really. How come no one knows this?"

"I know this."

"Ginny never mentioned it."

"I doubt Miss Ginny is aware of it. As I understand it, Ginny and Selena have not spoken to each other since the ice storm. How shall I say this . . . they are at odds with each other."

"I never saw an announcement in the newspaper."

"That's because they got married in Florida on the QT. Hardly anyone knows. They've kept it very quiet."

"Don't you think that's interesting?"

"I think that is very interesting. Especially since a wife does not have to testify against her husband in Kentucky unless we can make a deal with her."

"Believe me, if they were involved in Dwight's disappearance, it will be Farley who rolls over first." I looked around the dining room. "Are they here?"

"They still are in Lexington. One of my boys is keeping an eye on them. So far, Farley is at work and Selena is at home." He stood. "I'm going to trot down to the scene. If we should see each other later in the day, please act as though you don't know me. Okay?"

I made a face. "You should be so lucky."

As Goetz left the dining room, I made my way to the buffet table and loaded my plate. I sat at a table overlooking the Cumberland River and watched the birds at the feeding station. While stuffing my face, I pondered on the sad turn of events. I knew it had been a long shot, but I had still clung to the hope that Dwight was alive somewhere and would soon make his way home. Now

that sliver of hope was gone.
The eggs got stuck in my throat.

59

Ginny called my room and said officers from the State Police were in her room and would I come.

I didn't even wait for her to finish, but put the phone down and hurried to her room, which was just two doors down.

Quietly knocking on the door, I opened it and entered. There was Ginny sitting in a chair.

A female State Police officer sat opposite her while a large male officer waited near a wall.

The space was very small, making the room feel tight and suffocating.

I nodded to the officers and sat on the bed facing Ginny.

Ginny reached for my hand as she prepared herself for the worst.

The woman officer looked very sympathetically at Ginny.

"Anyone else coming?" asked the male officer.

Ginny shook her head. She didn't look up, but kept her eyes on the worn-out carpet covering the floor.

"Ma'am, is Dwight Marcum Wheelwright your son?"

Ginny gave a little moan.

I spoke on her behalf. "Yes, Officer."

The man directed his attention to me, as Ginny would not make eye contact with him. "Ma'am, we have reason to believe that the remains of Dwight Wheelwright have been found. We are very sorry for your loss."

"Are you positive?" I asked.

"We will have to conduct a DNA test to make a positive ID, but we are reasonably sure that the remains of Dwight Marcum Wheelwright have been discovered. His dental records match what we have found so far."

Ginny gave another little groan.

"Does Mrs. Wheelwright need to make an ID of the body?" I asked.

The two officers glanced at each other.

The woman spoke. "There is no need for that at this time."

"Can I see him?" squeaked Ginny, speaking for the first time.

"We are still in the recovery stage. This may take a while."

"Once you take him to the morgue, can I see him?"

The woman officer, whose badge identified her as Officer Clint, said with as much kindness as possible, "I don't think that is a good idea. You want to remember your son as he was." She then added. "You have done all you can. We will be as gentle with Dwight's remains as possible."

Ginny's eyes widened with concern.

"In fact," continued Officer Clint, "I think it might be a good idea that you went home and waited for word there. This might take us days to finish here and you would be more comfortable in your own home."

Ginny shook her head. "I want to wait at the recovery scene. My son needs me."

Officer Clint's sympathetic eyes begged me to help. She just didn't want to say what needed to be said.

I squeezed Ginny's hand. "Ginny, I think they are trying to tell you that Dwight's body is in a bad state of decomposition. It might take hours or days to work the site of his death."

Ginny let out a loud wail.

The male officer flinched, wanting nothing more than to get out of that small hotel room.

I wrote my cell number on a pad and handed it to Officer Clint. "Will you please keep us informed? I will stay with Mrs. Wheelwright."

Officer Clint handed me her card. "Please call me anytime. As soon as I am allowed, I will give you what information I can."

I nodded as she rose to leave. Turning my attention to Ginny, I didn't even hear the door close. "We are just in the way here. Let me take you home."

But Ginny didn't hear me. She was submerged in a deep and abiding sorrow.

There was nothing I could do but give testimony to her anguish. I sat in the chair opposite her and held Ginny's hand as she mourned the death of her only child.

Watching her reminded me of the famous words of the biblical King David lamenting the death of his beloved son, "Oh, Absalom. Absalom. My son, Absalom."

60

Matt knocked on my door hours later.

Ginny was resting, exhausted from crying. I was hoping that soon as she was able I could take her back to Lexington.

"What did you find out?" I asked Matt while pouring him a soft drink.

He took the glass and drank greedily and then held out the empty glass for more. Even though it was early spring, his face was burned from the sun. I got out several bottles of water for him as well. I was suspicious that Matt was dehydrated.

"I found Goetz and talked to him for a considerable period of time. I also spoke to the State Police. There was more reticence, but this is what I found out. There is no body to speak of. There are bones scattered in a two-square-mile grid, probably the work of animals. It's going to take time to legally determine cause of death, but the upper mandible was found along with most of the skull. It looks as though Dwight was killed by blunt force trauma."

"They really know for sure it's Dwight?"

Matt nodded. "They have already compared the teeth to Dwight's dental records and it seems like a fit even though some teeth are missing. There's still enough to ID him. Also, remnants of clothing were found. The description matches what his wife said he had on when he left. Scraps really, but enough to match." Matt paused for a moment. "There's blood on the clothing."

"So what now?"

"They will continue to search for any missing bones and teeth. Goetz is going back to Lexington tonight. I think he is going to get a subpoena for Dwight's house and business.

"Apparently Goetz has interviewed your Miss Darlene several times and could never shake her from the story that the man she checked out on the third was not Dwight, so he thinks that perhaps Dwight was killed in Lexington and Farley impersonated Dwight to make it look like he drowned."

I sat down on the bed with Matt. "Do you really think Selena and Farley might have had something to do with this?" I shook my head. "It's too horrible to contemplate, but it is one of my theories. I just don't want to believe it."

Matt wrapped his arms around me, pulling me down on the bed with him. "There, there, Rennie. Let it all out."

I was mentally and physically exhausted. I wanted to be back home at the Butterfly with Baby. I wanted my own bed. I didn't want to play nursemaid to a grieving mother. I wished Dwight was properly buried and the whole affair was done and over with.

But this was going to take months, even years, for a final conclusion.

My mind swirled with possible scenarios as tears leaked down my face onto Matt's chest.

What could have been the possible motive?

If Selena was involved, why would she kill her devoted husband?

Why did Dwight take her name off his life insurance policy?

Why did Amanda think something was wrong with Dwight several weeks before his death?

Why did Dwight want Farley to buy him out?

Why did Farley concoct that ridiculous story of Dwight having an affair with Susie Brinkman? He should have known it would be found out.

And where was the missing cashiers check for the initial down payment for the buyout to Dwight?

61

I must have fallen asleep. When I awoke, I was alone in the room. On the other double bed was a note from Matt that he was at the Falls. As soon as I awoke, I was to get him and we were all going back to Lexington.

I washed my face and combed my messy hair. My eyes were red and my nose looked swollen. I didn't give a damn. I was in mourning. Not wanting to run into other guests, I took the side door out to the parking lot and found Matt's car. It was just too long a walk to the Falls for me.

It only took several minutes to drive to the Falls and find a parking space. Using my cane, I cautiously descended the handicapped ramp onto the flat expanse of sandstone rocks bordering the Cumberland River.

At the rocks' edge stood Matt staring out at the water.

Carefully making my way on the rocks, I stood beside Matt, admiring the Cumberland River thunder over a ledge to form a pool where the river gathered itself and continued on its winding path to join the Ohio River. A brilliant rainbow formed at the base of the pool and curved upwards until it faded out into the mist.

"How can something so beautiful be so treacherous?" whispered Matt.

I didn't respond but just gazed upon the rushing green water spilling over the edge. "Let's go home, Matt," I pleaded. "There's nothing but death here."

"Your bag in the car?"

"Yes. All we have to do is pick up Ginny. I told her to be ready. She should be waiting in front of the lodge."

Matt took a deep breath. I could tell he wanted to go home. We turned together, making our way past mounds of little pebbles of coal deposited by the river. I had to be careful as the rock bed had depressions that might cause me to fall. Matt helped to guide me back to the handicapped ramp.

"Watch that hole, Josiah. Walk around it. It's not too much further," he said, gauging the distance to the parking lot. Suddenly he stopped and jerked me behind him. "Mother fu . . .!" he exclaimed.

An older couple passing us gave Matt a look of annoyance. The man started to say something, but his wife hushed him, pulling him down the pathway.

"What is it?" I cried, trying to look over his shoulder.

"I could have sworn that I just spotted O'nan."

"What?" Fear ran down my spine as I swiveled, glancing from tree to building to tree to car to parking lot. I started to tremble.

"Stay behind me," again cautioned Matt as he hurried to the parking lot.

A van of tourists had parked beside Matt's car, providing some cover while they gathered their things and untied a canoe from the top of the van.

This gave Matt ample time to check the inside of the car, the tires, and finally, after falling to his knees, the underside of the car.

I got in the back seat. Rummaging through my purse, I searched for my Taser.

Matt drove back to the lodge, following other cars all the time looking for O'nan. Once in Dupont Lodge's parking lot, he pulled out his phone and called Goetz, hoping to follow him back to Lexington.

Goetz answered on the first ring.

Matt quickly told him he was sure he had seen O'nan.

"Okay. Wait there and I will call the State Police and have them follow you out of the park. I've already started back, but I can meet you in Corbin and follow you up on I-75. That's the best I can do."

"What about O'nan?"

"I'll check into it. He has a court order requiring him to stay a hundred feet from Josiah. I don't think it was a coincidence that they were both at Cumberland Falls at the same time."

Goetz must have driven out of range, as Matt lost the connection. Scanning the parking lot, Matt rushed to

meet Ginny as she came out the side door with her bag.
Grabbing her arm, he pulled her to the car and practically
shoved her inside. Slamming her door shut, he hurried to
the driver's side and screeched out of the parking lot.

Ginny looked aghast. "What are you doing, Matt?
Slow down," she cried. "Slow down!"

Suddenly something slammed into the back left door,
making the car swerve. Ginny and I screamed as the
right front tire went over the side of the road, causing the
fender to scrape along the guardrail that divided the road
from a cliff.

Matt managed to keep control of the car and sped
along US 25 until he pulled into a gas station in Corbin.

Goetz was impatiently waiting for us. "Why didn't you
wait for the State Police? I just got a call from them."

Matt jumped out of the car and pointed. "That's why."

Goetz bent over and put his finger in a hole in the
back left door.

"What does that look like to you?" asked Matt. "I'm
sure you recognize a bullet hole when you see one!"

Scowling, Goetz got out his cell phone and dialed the
Lexington Police. "Put a APB on Fred O'nan. Proceed
with caution. Armed and dangerous. I think he just tried
to kill Josiah Reynolds again."

62

Exhausted, Detective Goetz unlocked the door to his apartment and staggered inside.

It had been a long two days, starting with waiting for the State Police to find Dwight Wheelwright's burial site. So far they had discovered much of his remains, but not ground zero. Then someone had taken a shot at Josiah Reynolds. Granted, she was a boil on his butt, but she didn't deserve to be gunned down.

In fact, she hadn't deserved much of the crap she had had to endure for the past five years. At times, Goetz really felt bad for Josiah. Truth be told, he liked her . . . even admired her, but every time he looked up, she was in his face poking her nose where it didn't belong.

It bothered him that O'nan hadn't been found yet. The guy was a nutter. Had always been a nutter.

Goetz had never liked him, even when O'nan had been a patrol officer. He had always thought that O'nan was a bad cop. He couldn't believe it when O'nan was promoted to the homicide division, but O'nan could schmooze people when he wanted something. Obviously he had schmoozed Goetz's superiors.

Goetz had always hated being witness to the pain associated with his job. He really felt for the families of the victims, but O'nan got off on it. Goetz could see it in O'nan's eyes. O'nan liked to see people suffer.

As soon as Josiah was tucked in at the Butterfly, Goetz had bothered some judges at their country clubs. He didn't care that it was Sunday. He didn't care if they were pissed about having to give up their evening golf games.

He wanted subpoenas. He wanted them bad. Goetz thought he could prove that Dwight was killed in his own house. And he thought he knew why. All he needed to find was a small trace of Dwight's blood.

Goetz and his boys would hit both Dwight's house and the office early the next morning.

But first he had arranged for Officer Snow to guard the Butterfly until O'nan could be found. That ass!!!

Yes, he was bone weary. He was going to fall into bed with his clothes on.

Goetz felt for the light switch, wishing he had left a living room light on, as it was dark in his apartment. It was then he smelled cigarette smoke.

"Eh, eh, eh. No touchy your gun, Goetz. That's it. Remain very still. Okay. It seems like I've got your attention."

"What are you doing here, Fred?"

"You and I are going to have a little talk."

Goetz tried to adjust his eyes to the darkness in the living room. All he could make out was a lighted cigarette across the room. O'nan must have drawn the drapes shut.

"I want you to close the door. That's it, nice and slow. Now take out your gun and throw it on the couch. Don't do anything stupid, Goetz. I've got a gun trained on you."

Goetz looked down and saw a red circle on his chest. He began to sweat. "Okay, Fred. Let's take it easy. I'm reaching into my jacket and pulling out my gun. Nice and easy, just like you said."

"Toss it on the couch, big man," demanded O'nan.

Goetz tossed his gun on the couch.

O'nan turned on a table lamp next to him. He was sitting in Goetz's TV chair with several empty bottles of beer rattling around on the floor.

"What are you doing here?" asked Goetz. He really wanted to punch the kid's face in.

"Before we start our little dance, I want you to stand over there . . . away from the door," said O'nan waving his gun. "That's good . . . there. Now I want you to sit on your hands on the floor."

"Aw, come on," griped Goetz, noticing that O'nan's gun had a silencer.

"Just do it, man. I've got nothing to lose if I shoot you."

"You've got plenty to lose. A murder rap. A murder of a cop, at that."

"Shut up. I'm gonna do the talking." O'nan pointed the gun at Goetz's feet. "Sit down or you're gonna be missing one of your toesies." O'nan grinned as he watched Goetz wrestle his big bulk onto the floor.

"Why did you go after Josiah Reynolds?"

"Did I get her?" asked O'nan.

Goetz could hear the sexual heat in O'nan's voice when he asked about Josiah. "Didn't even scratch her. I though you were a better shot than that."

"Damn," O'nan laughed. "That bitch has nine lives. That's why I'm here. I need your help."

Goetz sneered, "I wouldn't piss on you if you were on fire."

O'nan frowned. "That's such a worn out expression. Let's talk about something new and fresh. Something that will interest you. I mean really interest you." He held up a cheap little necklace and twirled it in the light.

Goetz caught his breath but kept his face neutral.

"She told me that Grandpa had gotten this for her." O'nan grinned again. "Cute little thing she is. What's her name . . . oh, yes, Dottie, short for Dorothy. That was your mother's name if I recall correctly."

Goetz remained stone faced. But inside, he was crumbling. Goetz was beginning to understand Josiah's deep, abiding fear of this man.

O'nan reached inside his shirt pocket. "And this is from Michael." O'nan held up a Pokemon card. "He says for me to say hi for him. Has a learning disability, doesn't he?" O'nan threw the items at Goetz's feet.

"They both live in different states. How did you . . .?"

O'nan wildly waved his gun while interrupting Goetz. He ranted, "Doesn't matter. The important thing for you to realize is I know where they live and obviously have access to them. And don't even try to warn your kids about me. They won't even see me coming. I have friends. Lots of friends who are only too happy to do things for me because I can buy them. I have lots of money, you see." O'nan chuckled. "If you've got money, you've got friends." He began to sing, "If you've got the money, honey, I've got the time. Now, who sang that? Goetz?"

Goetz mumbled, "Don't know."

O'nan leaned forward in his chair. "You knew my family had money. How do you think I could stay on the run for so long? My mother simply adores me and gives me lots and lots of it."

"If you touch anyone in my family, I'll kill you, Fred. I'll hunt you down. I swear it."

"You have forgotten our little talk at High Bridge last year. I told you then that I was going to be calling on you. Now everything has been set in place. If you don't do exactly what I say, one of your little darlings is going to get hurt. Perhaps a car will jump a curb and hit one of your little mewling kiddies or they'll go missing from their bed. Lots of terrible things can happen. But you do what you are told, everything will be okay. If you don't do what I say, things will get very bad for you, Goetz. Very bad indeed."

"Like that girl you raped and almost beat to death when you were sixteen. You didn't know that I knew about that," revealed Goetz.

"Those files were supposed to be expunged. How did you know?" O'nan's voice suddenly became strained and high-pitched.

"I took one of my vacations in your old hometown. Yeah, the files were expunged, but old timers like to talk. It only takes a twenty and information just spills forth. I can see why your family moved away. Not very well thought of. The old timers say that you were trouble from the get-go. I think one of them called you a bad seed."

"Goetz, if you're trying to get me angry, it's not going to work. I have the upper hand and know it. Not only will your family suffer, but I will make sure it comes out how you were skimming money when you were an undercover cop."

O'nan raised his gun and shot a family picture hanging above Goetz's head, scattering shards of glass. The report from the pistol was barely above a whisper as he fired.

Goetz shut his eyelids. Tiny shards of glass sprinkled his face and hair, threatening to fall into his eyes, cutting them if he opened them. He was effectively blind now and totally helpless.

"Now enough of the bull. You are going to do exactly what I tell you to do or you're gonna suffer, man, I mean really suffer. I will burn you. Burn the heart out of you."

O'nan leaned back in his chair and stared at the ceiling. "There has to be a reckoning. A reckoning with Josiah Reynolds," he hissed. "And you are going to help me, aren't you?"

O'nan snapped his head forward. "I didn't hear you. You are going to help me on my date with Professor Reynolds, aren't you?"

Goetz could not hide the hate and loathing in his voice that he had for his former partner, but he whispered, "Yes."

63

It was late at night when Goetz managed to find one of the last payphones in Lexington. He reluctantly inserted coins and dialed the number he had been given.

It rang a few times before someone picked up the phone on the other end.

"The coroner is finished with Dwight Wheelwright's remains. I just talked to his mother, Ginny. He is going to be buried in the family plot in Whitley County. There is going to be a ceremony four days from now. Mrs. Wheelwright and some of her friends are going down, including Josiah. She will be exposed outside and vulnerable. That will be the only time you will be able to get close to her," prompted Goetz, looking around to see if anyone noticed him.

"What did you tell her about me?" groused O'nan.

"I said you were spotted in Georgia. She thinks you are out of the state. She will feel safe to come out of the Butterfly, but you've only got one crack at this.

"Regardless of the outcome, Asa Reynolds will have operatives in Whitley County within forty-five minutes of picking up your trail. You better have an escape plan."

"Your concern touches me," O'nan mocked.

"I've done my part. Call off your boys. My family is in the clear."

"I think I'll keep them in my crosshairs until this is over. Just to be sure you're not double-crossing me."

"The thought never entered my mind."

The man on the other end chuckled. "Yeah. Sure," he said before hanging up.

Goetz slammed the phone back in its cradle. Taking out a handkerchief, he wiped off his fingerprints.

Getting back into his car, Goetz noticed that his hands were shaking. He leaned over to the glove compartment and pulled out a chrome-plated flask. Tilting the flask, he took a deep drink of bourbon. It burned going down. Goetz wiped his mouth with the back of his hand. He caught his reflection in the rearview mirror. His eyes were wide with apprehension.

This was not going to go down well. Not well at all.

64

"What are you doing here?" asked Matt. "We should be getting home."

"I thought I'd offer this flower wreath to the Falls," I remarked.

"An age-old custom. Ancient people used to throw precious items in the water as offerings to the gods," Matt said.

"No gods here," I mused. "They must have left town."

"It's late. We should go," cautioned Matt, anxiously glancing behind him. "Ginny's already heading back with her pastor."

"That was nice of him to come all the way down here and officiate at Dwight's funeral."

"We can talk about this in the car. Let's go," Matt urged.

"This is the part of the day that Kentuckians call the gloaming. Just a few minutes before twilight. Doesn't the light look beautiful . . . Matt, what is it?"

Matt had uttered a cry. He looked at me in surprise and then bent over before crumpling on the sandstone rocks that encapsulated the river.

"MATT! MATT!" I fell to my knees and tugged at Matt until I turned him over.

Blood bubbled from his mouth.

My hands felt sticky. Looking down, I saw that they were covered in blood.

"HELP! HELP!" I screamed.

No one heard me. The rushing of the water over the Cumberland Falls drowned out my cries.

That's when I saw him.

I saw O'nan coming toward me with a maniacal grin on his face. In his hand was a gun with a silencer.

Adrenaline can be a wonderful thing. I don't even remember how quickly I got to my feet and started running . . . but running where?

O'nan was between me and safety.

I ran back toward the river and the Falls.

I hadn't gone twelve feet before O'nan caught up with me. Grabbing the back of my coat collar, O'nan pulled me close to him so he could bring the gun up to my temple. "Did you miss me?" giggled O'nan into my ear.

I began twisting and flaying my arms, forcing O'nan to strike my head with his gun. It stunned me enough to stop resisting.

"Enough of that," scolded O'nan. "I'm not going to shoot you. That's too fast. I want you to experience fear until the very last nanosecond." He began dragging me over the rock ledge toward the Cumberland River.

If he threw me into the river, there would be no way I would be able to resist the massive force of the water going over the Falls.

"STOP! LET ME GO!" I screamed, trying to pull away, but O'nan was too strong. I felt the water fill my shoes as he began dragging me into the rushing current. "NO! NO!" I begged.

O'nan laughed.

He was going to do it. O'nan was actually going to kill me.

The hell he would!

I rammed my elbow into his gut.

Gasping, O'nan released his hold just time enough for me to wrench away. Sloshing through the water, I tried to make my way back to shore, but the current was too strong. The water kept threatening to pull my feet out from underneath me.

Oh my God! I was going to go over the Cumberland Falls.

O'nan crashed into me from behind, causing me to fall facedown in the water. He pushed my face into the muck of the river bottom.

I felt for a loose rock and then flayed my arms trying to pull O'nan off, but I was using up my oxygen. I began to lose consciousness.

I was dying.

Then . . . inexplicably, O'nan lifted his hands.

Gagging and coughing up water, I rose, scrambling for the riverbank. Looking behind me, I saw O'nan on his knees in the water looking surprised, just like Matt had looked before he had fallen.

O'nan glanced at his chest and then at me.

The water was red for a second before the current washed the blood away.

Grabbing onto a boulder, I watched as O'nan tried to say something to me. Then he fell over and was caught in the current.

O'nan swirled in an eddy before the current picked him up and carried him away. He dipped and bobbed as the water rushed over boulders and then finally to the edge.

O'nan was silent as he went over the Cumberland Falls.

65

Goetz removed the scope and wiped down the rifle before placing it in a canvas bag. Stooping over, he picked up several heavy rocks, placing them in the bag also.

He knew Asa Reynolds would be suspected of being behind the shooting, but he couldn't help that. Goetz hoped she had a good alibi.

Carefully, he emerged from his hiding spot on a rock outcrop across the river.

Taking one last look, Goetz saw Josiah crawl out of the water, making her way to her friend, Matt.

A man who had been walking his dog ran toward her. He frantically dialed 911 on his cell phone.

Satisfied that Josiah was getting help, Goetz made his way back to his vehicle. He was sure no one had seen him. After tossing the bag into the trunk, he carefully drove away, leaving the car lights off.

Using the back roads, Goetz drove to Laurel River Lake. Finding a deserted spot near where the lake was the deepest, Goetz made an offering of the rifle.

The lake accepted it.

66

I looked up to see Goetz tapping on the observation window of the ICU room. Like a rusty machine that needed oil, I struggled out of my chair by Matt's bed and went out into the hallway.

"How's he doing?" asked Goetz.

I shrugged. "He's still in a coma. It's touch and go."

"I see that he's still on life support."

"Yeah."

"Come over and sit down. I want to tell you what has happened." Goetz gave me a stern look. "Are you up to it? You've been here for three days. You look like hell."

I smiled bitterly. "I can always count on you to make me feel better."

Goetz helped me to a large waiting room. There were only a few people as it was after 1 a.m. We sat in a corner.

"You were right. Farley rolled over on Selena."

I nodded.

"Apparently, they had been having an affair for some time. Somehow Dwight became suspicious. It was the reason that he wanted to leave the business. When Farley gave him guff about the selling price, Dwight decided to confront them both. The fishing trip was a ruse. Dwight waited to see if he could catch them together and he did . . . at his house."

"That's why he took Selena's name off the insurance policy, but he never told her," I offered.

"Probably hadn't had the opportunity to tell her." Goetz glanced about to see if anyone was listening. "Anyway, apparently Dwight walked in on them in the dining room. There were accusations. Dwight was furious, so he threw a punch at Farley."

"So Farley picked up the chocolate centerpiece and killed Dwight with it."

Goetz shook his head. "This is where it gets screwy. Farley did hit Dwight with the chocolate, stunning him. But it was Selena who actually killed Dwight. She got a knife from the kitchen and stabbed Dwight to death."

"Good God!" was all I could say.

"Now they have to hide the body, so Farley came up with the plan to make it look like Dwight had drowned in Laurel Lake."

"But he really buried Dwight in the forest."

277

"Right on."

"What about the scorpion bite?"

"Farley was stung, but had antibiotics at home from a previous injury and just "manned-up" as they say. He didn't get any medical help. Said the scorpion just about did him in, but he looked up scorpion bites on the Internet and did what the website recommended.

"What about the missing check for the two hundred grand?"

"Neither Selena nor Farley knew what Dwight did with the check."

I was about to ask about the confusion of the location of Dwight's wallet when I realized I didn't give a damn anymore. It would probably come out in the trial. I could wait until then.

"Let me take you home, Josiah," offered Goetz gently. "You're not doing Matt any good by getting sick yourself. You can barely keep your eyes open."

I just sat. I was numb.

"That's it." Goetz stood up. "Wait right here." He came back a few minutes later with my coat and purse. "Let's go," he barked, pulling me to my feet. He wrapped the coat around my shoulders and put his arm around my waist, helping me to walk. "I'll call the DA and ask them to put off your interview for a while. You're in no shape to talk to anyone until you get your head clear."

"Is it really over?" I asked.

Goetz knew what I was talking about. "He is really dead, Josiah. You don't have to be scared anymore."

Nothing else was said as we walked out of the hospital into the chilly night.

Epilogue

"My name is Josiah Reynolds. I used to be an art professor at the University of Kentucky. Now I make my living from honeybees, selling honey at a local farmers' market.

"I live in the Butterfly, which sits on a cliff overlooking the Kentucky River. I am a widow.

"I have one child–Asa. She had worked for the Secret Service until she reported abuses within the department. Now she works as an independent contractor. Interpret that as you will.

"Did she assassinate O'nan? I don't know and I'm never going to ask.

"The New Scotland Yard has already questioned Asa in London. Apparently she was in Rome at the time on an assignment. So unless my daughter can be in two places at one time, you can rule her out. I'm sure they have already reported to you, so why are you asking me?

"You can grill me with all the questions you want, but I'm not going to say one more word until my lawyer, Shaneika Mary Todd, arrives. I've learned how to deal with cops. I can't believe that you are pestering me with questions right now.

"I'm just going to sit right here . . . and try to block out the fact that Kentucky is thirsty for the blood of her sons. She demands sacrifices, just like Chief Dragging Canoe had warned Daniel Boone."

*

In the beautiful and seductive land of Caintuck, the past is never past and the thirst of the rich dark earth is never quenched.

Bonus Chapters

DEATH BY HAUNTING
A JOSIAH REYNOLDS MYSTERY

&

LAST CHANCE MOTEL
A ROMANCE NOVEL

DEATH BY HAUNTING
A Josiah Reynolds Mystery

Prologue

Mr. Bailey, who lived up Tates Creek Road from Josiah Reynolds, was awakened in the wee hours of the night to find that his covers had been pulled off. His growling Jack Russell terrier and clinging orange tabby were lying so close to him as to be almost pushing Mr. Bailey off his new mattress.

"What the . . .?" muttered Mr. Bailey, as he turned to push the cat away and question his wife of forty-seven years. "Mavis! What's going on?" asked Mr. Bailey, as he turned on his side to find his missus wide-eyed and sitting straight up against the headboard of their new poster bed, staring into a darkened corner of their bedroom.

Mavis pointed toward the corner and croaked, "Mama's here."

Mr. Bailey followed his wife's outstretched hand pointing to a dark corner where indeed stood his mother-in-law, Cordelia Sharp, wearing her favorite blue seersucker summer dress and lavender wig.

The only problem was that Cordelia Sharp had been dead for seven years.

1

My name is Josiah Reynolds. I was named for the Hebrew king in the Old Testament.

Old King Josiah purified the Temple from idolatry and cult prostitution. He ordered that all the priests who followed the pagan gods and goddesses be killed.

To be sure it was the King's way or the highway, buddy, for if his soldiers caught up with you, it meant an unpleasant death.

I am a widow-woman and until recently was the object of an extreme stalker who ended up falling over the Cumberland Falls and crashing on the rocks below. But not before the creep had shot my dog and two of my friends, one of whom is still fighting for his life.

But going over the Falls is not how he died. Someone put a bullet through his chest as he was trying to drown me in the Cumberland River.

I don't know who killed my nemesis, O'nan, and I really don't give a rat's . . . well, you know. I'm just glad he's dead.

My daughter swore on the Bible it was not she. I made her put her hand on the Good Book and swear an oath to me. I hope she is Southern enough to believe that if she lied, she will be cursed. But that doesn't mean she couldn't have had someone else do it for her.

I have a few other names in the hat, but I really don't care except that I am left with the repercussions of O'nan's actions. And none of the subsequent decisions are easy.

2

It was one of the worst decisions I had ever had to make, but I thought it the right one. I just had to tell Franklin. He would have a fit and there was a strong possibility he might never forgive me, but it had to be done. I would tell him later as I had to stop by the Big House first since I had gotten a call from my next-door neighbor, Lady Elsmere.

Lady Elsmere, aka June Webster from Monkey's Eyebrow, Kentucky had the penchant for marrying wealthy men who died at an early age. Widowed twice, she was as rich as Midas and had come back to her Kentucky roots after living in England for several decades. She had been my friend for many years and she helped my deceased husband with his career by letting him restore her antebellum home, which is still a showstopper in the Bluegrass.

I call her home the Big House. Both Lady Elsmere and I liked to pretend that we lived in a Tennessee Williams' play. Very often, we are not wrong.

After pushing in the code for the massive steel front gate, I drove up the pin oak-lined driveway and parked in the back of the house so I could go into the servants' entrance where there were no steps.

I no longer relied on my cane, but why tempt fate? You see I had had a terrible fall. I fell off an eighty-foot cliff, crashing into a ledge midway down. The fall busted my face, most of my teeth, lots of bones, and my pride. As a result, I limp, wear a hearing aid, and pee on myself every time I burp.

On the positive side, I am no longer fat and when they were reconstructing my face, the docs gave me a little helpful boost in the age department. I look younger than I am, and my new teeth are so bright, they positively glow in the dark. I never need a flashlight anymore. I just smile.

To tell you the truth, I am held together with spit and a prayer.

I tried the door. Of course, it was unlocked.

When would June realize that she and her staff could no longer live like it was 1959 when no one in Lexington locked their doors?

I entered through the mudroom, sat on a bench and took off my snow boots, putting on the slippers I had brought with me.

We had recently had a late snowstorm just when the fruit trees were blooming. Weather in Kentucky can be freakish at times as winter in Kentucky yields to spring begrudgingly.

While hanging up my coat, Bess poked her head in and said, "Just wanted to see who came a'callin'."

"Bess, you really need to start locking the doors. Anyone could have come in."

"You're so right. So right. There's a lot of meanness in the world."

"You're not gonna start locking the back door, are you?" I complained, giving a look of consternation and following her into the kitchen.

Bess laughed while beating egg whites into a meringue. "Nope. Tired of living in fear. O'nan is dead and like the Israelites . . . we are set free."

"There are other bad people out there, Bess," I said, giving her a big hug from behind. "Remember that boy who tried to steal your Christmas jewels?"

"Get off with you," laughed Bess. "Can't you see that I'm in the middle of making a masterpiece here?"

"Where are Charles and your mama?"

"Mummy went to Charleston to see her people and you know, where Mummy goes, so does Daddy. She wanted to show off her new jewelry that June gave her for Christmas."

"Who's doing the butler stuff?"

"Liam." Bess poured the stiff whites on the chocolate pies. "He's not half bad . . . when he's not under the weather."

"Is that what we are calling him now?" I asked, as Liam had been known as Giles until recently.

It seems that Liam Doyle had been a thief by profession in another life and the Irishman had been hiding from the police under the disguise of an English valet. I guess his past had been ironed out as he was using his real name and that Lady Elsmere had decided to keep him. I know it's hard to keep up with all of this.

Bess nodded while still beating the egg whites.

I waited for her to say more about Giles, I mean, Liam, but she was silent. Darn! I continued, "That's good. Maybe Charles and your mother can retire then."

"June said . . . I mean Lady Elsmere," teased Bess, giving a wicked grin, "that Daddy can't retire from the Big House until she's dead and buried in the ground."

"That may not be for some time."

Bess torched the whites with a kitchen blowtorch darkening the edges. "She'll outlive us all. She's having too much fun to die."

"I know that things have been tried in the past to help lessen the strain on your daddy."

"Part of the problem is that Daddy misses the house when he's not in charge and thinks no one can do as good a job."

"And he is right. No one takes care of this house like Charles but he's got to oversee the farm, take care of June's charities plus he's on the board of the Humane Society. That's way too much for anybody. June can't live forever."

"Who says I can't?" demanded June, walking into the massive kitchen. "Are you trying to shove me into the grave, naughty girl?"

"NOOOO. We were just talking about how you make Charles' life miserable."

"Pshaww. Charles lives to complain. It's one of his little endearing qualities. Right Bess?"

Shaking her head, Bess turned to study her pies. "If you say so, Miss June, but Daddy's not getting any younger."

"I do say so," Miss June replied, giving me a long sideways glance. "Now what do you want? I just loaned Miss Eunice my best silver for some wedding reception you're having at your place. Have you come to collect it?"

"If you get one of the boys to put it in my car, I'll take it. However, you called me—remember?"

June started down the hallway. "What terrible weather to have a wedding reception. Just think of it. Suppose to be in the seventies next week. I guess the tornadoes will follow. They love to come with the spring rainstorms."

"June, what are you rattling on about?"

"The weather. Everyone talks about the weather. Ahem."

"I looked up and saw that June was standing in front of a newly acquired painting, hanging in the hallway by the grand staircase.

On the wall hung an oil painting of eight riders on horses racing beneath a dramatic stormy sky. It was gorgeous.

I leaned toward it. Were the horses in a race or were the riders exercising the horses and racing against the storm to get back to the barn? No, they had to be in a race as the riders were wearing silks. Looking for the name, I spied the "John Hancock" of John Henry Rouson.

"John Henry Rouson," I mumbled out loud. "Never heard of him."

"Oh my dear, he is very famous or was. Lord Elsmere actually introduced us in England."

"I'm not much into equine art."

"Living in Kentucky and you don't know who the famous horse painters are? I can't believe that I have found a topic that I know more than you." June tapped her foot. "Well, what do you think of it?"

"I think it's gorgeous. Where did you get it?"

"From Jean Louis. He brought his entire collection with him to Kentucky while he's working on my portrait. He said he couldn't bear not to see them even one day. Isn't that quaint?"

"Suspicious is what I call it. If he can't part with them, why did he give you one?"

"Oh, don't be such a gloomy cuss. Not everyone is on the make."

"How much did you pay for it?"

"It was a gift. See there."

I gave the painting a curious look.

Lady Elsmere continued, "He saw me admiring it and just gave it to me. Come. Come. You must see my new portrait. Of course, it's not done . . . just the bones . . . but it's wonderful. So like me."

I followed June down the hallway to the library. She opened the door.

Inside I smelled oil paint, turpentine, and the raw material of canvas. There were tarps thrown on the antique parquet floor in order to accommodate the huge wooden easel holding a very large canvas.

Behind the easel was Jean Louis puttering. He poked his head around. "Ah, bonjour mes amies." He waved his outstretched hand at us. "Entré s'il vous plait. I was just cleaning my brushes."

"I hope we're not intruding," said June.

"Lady Elsmere, you are never a bother. I see you bring the beautiful Josiah with you. Please come in. Madame Josiah, you have not come to visit me lately. Makes me think you don't like me. Oui?"

"I've been busy with a sick friend."

"Yes. Yes. It happened right after I arrived. Your friend, Monsieur Mathew Garth. He was shot, no?"

"Yes, and he is still gravely ill."

Jean Louis pursed his lips. "So sad when someone is so young."

"Yes, very sad for everyone."

"But the bad man is dead, n'est-ce pas?"

"So they tell me," I replied. I didn't like to talk about O'nan. He had been a rogue cop who had stalked me for several years, making my life a living hell.

"But I forget my manners, please sit. Lady Elsmere, might we have tea?"

"Of course. Please pull that rope for the butler."

"I'll take care of it," I announced, opening the library door. I poked my head out the hallway and yelled, "Hey Bess, can we have some tea?"

"Yeah, give me a minute or two," she yelled back.

"Okay." I closed the door. "It will be a minute or two," I deadpanned. Yes, I did that just to be a stinker.

Lady Elsmere squinted at me with fury while Jean Louis twiddled with his mustache looking amused.

I smiled sweetly and sat down on a couch in front of the portrait.

I hated when Lady Elsmere put on airs. After all, she was just June Webster from Monkey's Eyebrow, Kentucky and was raised on a farm, shoveling horse manure like most of her generation. The only reason she had money was that her first husband was a genius and had invented some doohickey in his garage, which made them both rich. He died of a heart attack while they were touring Europe and she then married Lord Elsmere, who was in need of a Lady, but didn't necessarily "need" a lady, if you know what I mean.

"So this is the painting," I drawled without
enthusiasm. "She already has two. The head and
shoulders over the fireplace in her bedroom and the full
length portrait in the dining room."

"Yes, but this is one of a woman in the full bloom of
her maturity," replied Jean Louis.

"You mean ancient," I quipped.

"Really, Josiah, I don't see why you are being so
unpleasant this afternoon. If I want another portrait,
what business is that of yours?"

I felt the heat rise to my cheeks. I *was* being awful.
"I'm sorry, June. My apologies, Jean Louis. I just had to
make a difficult decision and I'm afraid that I am taking it
out on the both of you. I'm so sorry. Really, I am."

June gasped, "You didn't pull the plug on Matt, did
you?"

"Of course not."

"Oh, goodness. Just for a moment I thought you had
. . . well, you know."

"Matt is doing better, but recuperation is going to take
longer than expected. The bullet ricocheted in his body,
hitting some vital organs." I threw my hands up and
stammered, "I . . . I hate to even talk about it. Again, my
apologies for being a tyrant."

"It is reasonable, Madame, that you wish to express
your anger at the injustice of the situation in which you
find yourself. However, maybe Lady Elsmere and I can
take your mind off your difficulty at least for a few
minutes."

June sat beside me and patted my hand. "Jean Louis is right. Let's talk about something else for awhile and take your mind off your troubles."

I smiled kindly at June.

She clapped her wrinkled hands. "Let's talk about my portrait. What do you think?"

Wearily I focused on the life-sized portrait of June complete with tiara, diamond necklace, bracelet, and rings. I had to admit it was stunning and June looked rather . . . majestic.

The background was very dark which emphasized a shimmering yellow organza ball gown, which June wore sitting with her hands folded on her lap. While her face portrayed an expression of serene countenance, it was her eyes that caught the viewer's interest. They seemed so animated that one might say a fire was emanating from them.

"Ummm. You look rather regal."

"Really? So you like it?" asked June.

"Now where is this painting going?"

"After my death, the University of Kentucky Medical Center will receive a large endowment . . . and this portrait as well."

"So it is going to be hung in public then." I stared at the portrait not knowing how to say it. Surely she must know.

"June, I think it's lovely, but don't you think it looks quite similar to the 1954 portrait of Queen Elizabeth by Sir William Dargie. You know, the one where she is wearing a yellow gown and now hangs in the Australian

Parliament. I mean . . . except for the face, they are almost identical."

"Oh, Lizzie won't mind."

"Lizzie. You call the Queen Lizzie? I didn't know that was a pet name for Her Majesty."

At that moment the door opened and in weaved Liam carrying a tea tray. "Shall I pour, Madam?" asked Liam.

"No thank you. Josiah can do that."

I made a face, as I disliked being conscripted to perform such tasks. The strength in my hands sometimes gave out without notice, causing me to drop things.

Seeing my discomfort, Jean Louis spoke up. "Put it by me, Liam. I'll pour for the ladies."

"Very good, Sir." Liam put the tea tray on a small table near us and left quickly, but not before I caught a whiff of whisky on him.

I stood up. "You must excuse me. It has been a long day and I'm very tired. Shall we do this another time?"

"Naturellement," replied Jean Louis, fluttering his pudgy hands.

"I'll walk you out," suggested June giving me a concerned look. "You do look tired, Josiah."

"You stay and enjoy your tea. My car is out back. No need for you to walk all that distance."

"Alright, but don't forget that I will pick you up tomorrow morning at 10:30 sharp."

I gave a blank look.

"For Terrence Bailey's memorial."

"Oh dear, I forgot. I promised Eunice that I would help her with the reception."

"I'll send Bess over to help Eunice. You go with me. Mavis would consider it a slight if we didn't show up, being neighbors and all."

"Won't she consider it a slight if Bess doesn't come?"

"Naw, she never liked Bess. Something about an ingredient being left out of a recipe that Bess was supposed to have given her years ago."

"Okay, I'll be ready, but I can't stay forever. I must be home by one."

June looked disappointed. She loved a good funeral and usually was the last to leave the wake. I think it was because she had a fondness for Jell-O casseroles. At least one person usually brought Jell-O, especially if they were over the age of sixty.

I gave a goodbye nod to Jean Louis and made my way out of the Big House, but not before Bess gave me one of her chocolate pies.

Gratefully, I accepted it. I was going to use it as a peace offering to Eunice when I told her I was going to a funeral in the morning, instead of helping her.

I just hoped it was not going to be thrown back in my face.

3

Since I didn't have the stamina to stand in long lines and June teetered as though she was going to fall over any moment, we both sat until the receiving line had thinned out.

The funeral had turned out to be a visitation. The funeral was the next day. I felt stupid sitting all dressed up in my widow weeds, but June loved the drama of it all.

Seeing that Mavis was getting tired of standing too, her daughter deposited her next to us. "Josiah, can you keep an eye on Mama for me?" she asked before joining her husband who was having much too good a time seeing old friends.

"No problem," I replied.

The daughter gave me a faint smile before returning to her father's casket.

"Not like the old days is it, Mavis," croaked June, "when we used to place our dead in the living room until the funeral?"

"It got to be too much if they died during the summer," mused Mavis.

Both ladies cackled.

"I remember sitting up all night with my grandmother before they put her in the ground," recalled June.

"Why did you do that?" I asked.

Both old crones looked at me as a rather pretty but stupid pet.

"Robbers," said Mavis. "They'd steal in your house and take the jewelry right off the dead."

"Sometimes, they even take the bodies and sell them to medical facilities," chimed in June.

"This sounds very Dickensian to me," I challenged.

"Only uptown people could afford to let the funeral home keep the bodies until the burial, and even then, a family member would stay to keep an eye on the funeral home staff.

"In the deep South, the staff would cut the hair and fingernails of the deceased and sell it the voodoo priests. Sometimes even cut off fingers to use in dark magic," detailed June.

Mavis nodded in agreement.

"Whatever," I murmured.

June went on. "I hope it's my first husband who comes for me when my time comes. I miss him so."

I countered. "I thought the love of your life was Arthur . . ."

"Shush," hissed June. "The dead do come for you."

Mavis sniffed. "Oh, I see that Josiah is too educated to believe in the old ways, but I can tell you first hand that Terrence died after Mama came for him."

June grabbed Mavis' gnarled hands. "Really. Your mother came for him?"

I snorted with derision. I don't know why. Hadn't Brannon come for me after I had fallen off the cliff and was near death? Why was I being such a booger? Guess, I'm ornery, that's all.

Both women looked at me with scorn.

"Tell me what happened, Mavis. I've got to know if there's an afterlife. I'll be going soon myself and it would be a comfort to know that a loved one would come for me."

"That's just it, June. Terry hated Mama. She always berated him while living. I think it was just an odd choice to send her."

I bit my tongue trying to be diplomatic for once. I wanted to know why Mavis didn't think her mother had come for her. "You said it had been a struggle for the longest time. What do you mean by that?" I asked.

Mavis blew her nose in an overused hanky. "Something was bothering him. Something fierce, but he wouldn't tell me what it was. It started after your

Valentine party, June. He was happy when we got there and then jumpy afterwards."

I suddenly became interested, as the purpose of the Valentine party was to introduce Jean Louis to Bluegrass society.

I didn't like Jean Louis. His lips said one thing, but his eyes said something else. Jean Louis was always asking questions, snooping.

Hey! Wait a minute. That sounds like me.

I didn't trust him and had been keeping an eye on him until Matt had been shot, then gave up. I had other priorities.

"What do you think was bothering him, Mavis?" asked June, greatly concerned. "Did someone say something to Terry that upset him? Had you been catin' around on him?"

Mavis gave a brief smile at the last suggestion. "What a ridiculous idea at my age!" She shook her head. "Like I said, he wouldn't tell me."

"Can you pinpoint exactly during the party when Terry became upset," I asked. "It might be important."

Mavis put a finger to her lips in thought. "Well, I was talking to Mrs. Dupuy about the robbery at Christmas when Terry interrupted us, saying he wanted to go home. He was very insistent."

"What had he been doing?"

Mavis spoke to June. "You know how he loved art. He was going to each of the rooms that were open for the party and looking at the artwork, saving the library for the last to see your portrait. Of course, the portrait wasn't finished, but he wanted to see the sketching on the canvas."

"Was he coming from the library?" I inquired.

"He was coming from the direction of the library, but I first saw him near the staircase," recounted Mavis, closing her eyes to help her remember the scene. "But I can't tell you for sure if he had been in the library."

"And?" I prompted.

"It wasn't too long after that Mother started showing up at night. Oh, it gave us both a terrible fright. We weren't sure what she wanted. She would never say. Just stand in the corner of the bedroom looking . . . this is terrible to say about one's own mother, creepy. She was creepy."

"To say the least," comforted June.

"It turned out she wanted Terry as he had a heart attack several weeks after the haunting." Mavis blew her nose again. "You'd think she'd come for me. I'm her blood."

"She might still, Mavis," I predicted.

Mavis jerked her head up. "Oh?" She didn't like that idea at all.

"What did Terry do between the party and your mother's appearance?" I asked.

"He was on the Internet constantly and then going to the library looking up old newspaper stories." Mavis blew her nose again.

"Do you know what about?" questioned June, handing Mavis a hanky from her purse.

Mavis was becoming somewhat untidy with all the nose blowing. She wiped her nose, looking at the both of us with wide, red-rimmed brown eyes that glistened with unspent tears. "Yes. He was investigating art thefts."

I started to ask about this when Mavis' son-in-law came to fetch her.

It was not the right time to question Mavis. The subject of art theft had certainly gotten my attention. That was a bone this dog would definitely dig up.

Last Chance Motel
A Romance Novel

Eva gazed into the floor-length mirror and was pleased with her reflection. The black negligee she had recently purchased encased her trim body like a glove. Her auburn hair glimmered with highlights and her skin looked like butter cream. Even though she was forty, Eva looked younger and worked at it.

Hoping that her sexy look might heat up her husband, who seemed a little frost-bitten lately, she put on the finishing touch. Passion Fire Red lipstick!

Nine years ago, she had met Dennis while helping his company remodel an old warehouse on the west side of Manhattan. Her boss had put Eva in charge of the cosmetic rehab of the warehouse while others dealt with structural issues. That was okay with Eva. Buying furniture and picking out paint colors was fun and she was given a huge budget with which to play.

It was at a briefing that Eva was introduced to Dennis, a junior executive at that time. He was to be the company's liaison with her.

There was instant chemistry and before long they were embroiled in a passionate affair, which spilled over into marriage two months after the project was completed.

Nine years. Eva shook her head in disbelief. Where had the time gone? Six of those years had been fantastic, but things started slipping three years ago.

It had begun when Eva and Dennis purchased an abandoned brownstone in Brooklyn near the Verrazano Bridge. They had been giddy when they first received the keys from the bank and began restoring the four-story brownstone, but things started taking a downward turn six months into the project.

To save money, Eva and Dennis decided to complete many of the cosmetic projects themselves. After working long hours at their firms, they would hurry home to the brownstone and work late into the night trying to tile the bathrooms or lay down bamboo floors or paint twelve foot ceilings. What started as fun became a strain both physically and mentally.

They began snapping at each other and it didn't take long to realize that they both had different visions for the brownstone, which created even more tension.

Eva wanted to restore the brownstone to its authentic former glory while Dennis wanted to gut and modernize it completely.

Dennis won.

When the brownstone was completed, Eva had to admit it was stunning, complete with all modern amenities. But to Eva, the brownstone was cold and void of any personality, but it was what Dennis liked. She disliked the cold paint colors he had chosen and the minimalist look of each room.

Eva realized that compromise was the cornerstone of marriage and wanted Dennis to be happy. That was very important to her. She could live with the renovation.

Now that the brownstone was finished, Eva wanted to heat up her faltering relationship with her husband and get it back on track.

Eva masked her irritation when Dennis finally got home . . . late as usual during the past seven months. Hearing the elevator rise to the master bedroom floor, Eva waited in the alcove trying to look sexy in her negligee.

The elevator reached the top and the door swung open. Dennis was going through the mail and barely looked up.

"Hello there, big boy," teased Eva.

Dennis looked up and froze when he saw Eva.

Eva noticed his hesitation and it threw her off her game. She suddenly felt foolish.

"What's up with you?" asked Dennis.

Eva, determined that the night be a success, smiled. "I thought we would celebrate your new promotion and the completion of the house. I have made a very nice dinner for us and then for dessert . . ."

"We celebrated last Saturday with our friends," retorted Dennis. He looked frustrated and a bit embarrassed.

"Yes, but I thought we could have a private celebration, just you and me," rejoined Eva.

Uh oh. This was not going as planned.

"Honey, I'm tired. I just want to eat and go to bed."

"Long day at the office?"

Dennis looked at the letters in his hand. His face was flushed. "Something like that."

"I have something that will make you feel better," chirped Eva. She was going to hit this out of the ballpark. Eva handed him two airline tickets.

"What's this?" Dennis asked, staring blankly at the tickets.

"I purchased two tickets to Miami for this weekend. The two of us on a getaway. No work. No house to think about. Just warm breezes and blue water. We can rent a boat and . . ."

"NO!"

"No?" echoed Eva. Her heart began to sink. Something was very wrong.

"This has got to end," Dennis said, cutting in, letting the mail fall to the floor. He looked at Eva as though he was looking through her. "I'm sorry I have let this go on for so long, but things have got to change."

Alarmed, Eva tried to hug Dennis but he pushed her away. Eva gasped. "What is it, Dennis? What's wrong? Are you ill?" She felt a numbing fear move up her spine.

"I'm sorry, Eva, but I'm not going anywhere with you. This is very hard to say, but I. . . I want a divorce."

Eva felt like a bullet had passed through her. "What? For heaven's sake, why? We have everything. We worked so hard on this house. Why Dennis? Why?"

"I don't love you anymore. That's why."

2

"Mr. Reardon wants the brownstone," demanded Dennis' lawyer.

Eva and her attorney sat across the conference table. "Where is Dennis?" Eva asked. Turning to her lawyer, she questioned, "Shouldn't Dennis be here?"

"Mr. Reardon has given me instructions to act on his behalf and feels his presence is not necessary under the circumstances."

"What circumstances? Not seeing me?" Eva asked.

"Eva," cautioned her lawyer. "Let me handle this."

"What circumstances are you referring to?" Eva asked again.

"I believe that Mr. Reardon has expressed concern about you being abusive lately."

Eva snorted in derision.

"Many women become upset when asked for a divorce and given no reason. Mrs. Reardon has been a faithful and constant companion to Mr. Reardon. I think that under the circumstances most women would raise their voices and maybe even throw some objects. It's human nature."

"Mr. Reardon feared for his life."

"Oh, please," scoffed Eva. "Give me a break."

"If Mr. Reardon feared for his safety he should have called the police and filed a complaint. Since there is no complaint, let's move on, shall we. Alleging that Mrs. Reardon is a threat without proof is counter-productive to your client's requests."

"Demands," rebuffed Dennis' lawyer.

"What are they?" asked Eva's attorney, putting a pencil to a legal pad.

"Quite simply, Mr. Reardon wants the brownstone." Dennis' attorney raised his hand. "I have been authorized to offer eight hundred thousand for your half, Mrs. Reardon, plus half of all moneyed accounts that you share with Mr. Reardon. I think it is a very equitable division of assets."

"I don't understand why Dennis would want the brownstone. It's too large for one person. I thought we were going to sell it and divide the proceeds," remarked Eva.

"They think that they . . ." the lawyer stopped suddenly, looking aghast at his faux pas.

"They?" questioned Eva.

"I meant he," stated Dennis' lawyer.

"You said 'they'."

Shaken, Eva leaned back in her seat. "They. That explains a lot. It's the missing piece of the puzzle of why he left me." She began to sob quietly.

Her lawyer closed his notebook. "Tell Mr. Reardon that Mrs. Reardon wants 1.2 million plus half of all the other assets or we are going to drag this out indefinitely."

"Oh no, you can't do that," complained Dennis' attorney. "The house needs to be available by the next several months before the . . ."

Both Eva and her lawyer's mouth dropped open at the implication of the statement.

Eva began to wail out loud.

Her lawyer stood and helped Eva to her feet. "I assume that Mr. Reardon's new friend is pregnant then. He'll meet our demands or I'll tie up that brownstone for years."

"Oh God," whispered Eva, being led from the conference room. "He's got a new woman and they're going to have a baby in my house. My house! I painted every room! I installed the tile! I refinished the wood floors!" She yelled, "This just went from bad to the absolute worst. He told me he didn't want any children."

Eva grabbed a woman in the hallway. "He said he would love me forever."

"They all say that, dearie. But if they can afford it, they trade us in every ten years or so for a new model. Once the tits start to sag, it's over," replied the stranger in sympathy. "We've all been there. It's just your turn now."

"What happened to true love?" murmured Eva.

Her lawyer snickered. "Surely you don't believe in that crap, do you? Just get the money and run."

"But I do. I do believe in true love," blurted Eva and she cried this mantra all the way home, that night and for the next several days until her body became so dehydrated she couldn't cry anymore.

3

Three months later, Eva signed the divorce papers and slipped them in the stamped mailer as directed. Licking the flap, she closed the mailer with a large sigh. "Well, that's the end of that," she said.

She hurried downstairs so she could catch the mailman whose truck she saw from the window. She caught him coming up the stoop and handed him the mailer.

Giving her a startled look, the mailman grabbed the envelope and hustled down the steps.

"I'm not that bad," she groused, noticing his reluctance to stay and chat.

A mother pushing a stroller hurried by when the toddler saw Eva and started to cry.

"Oh, come on now," complained Eva. Defeated, she pulled back inside the brownstone and looked in the hall mirror. "Jeez." Eva tried to flatten messy hair that would give Medusa a run for her money. Her eyes were sunken, teeth were yellow and dirty, and her skin was sallow.

Her outfit was pajamas that had not left Eva's body for the past two weeks and were straining at the seams as her new diet consisted of chocolate ice cream . . . and then strawberry ice cream . . . and again chocolate ice cream. With chocolate syrup. For a dessert, she inhaled Reddi-wip from the can.

And she stank.

"I'm in some deep, deep doo-doo," lamented Eva looking in the mirror and repelled by what she saw. "You're made of better stuff than this. You're just forty. Only six months ago you were hot stuff." She pulled on her belly fat. "Crap. I'm middle-aged now. The bloom has faded."

She gave the mirror one last pathetic look. "I just can't stop living. This is just a bump in the road." She took another hard look at herself. "Oh, who am I kidding? This is a freakin' firestorm!"

Coming to the realization that she had to battle her depression, Eva climbed the staircase to the third floor. There she took a long shower, washed her hair, shaved her legs, and put on some clean underwear. Looking around the bedroom, she found a pair of clean flannel pj's and a tee shirt. To complete the outfit, she slipped on some beat-up flip-flops.

Hungry, she went to the kitchen, but found nothing in the fridge to eat. Frustrated, she began looking for carryout menus when she spotted the airline tickets to Florida.

Eva bit her lip as tears clouded her eyes. "I'm not going to cry," she whispered. "All that is over. I'm going to buck up and get over this. I'm going to get a new life."

Staring at the plane tickets, Eva suddenly called her travel agent and ordered a new ticket to be waiting for her at the airport. Then Eva grabbed her coat and purse as she fled the brownstone.

Giving the brownstone one last look, Eva flipped the house key down a street grate.

Dennis would be surprised to discover that Eva had had the locks changed and she had just thrown the only front door key into the New York City sewer system.

Eva felt an immediate sense of relief.

Hailing a cab, she instructed the driver, "JFK please, and step on it."

Abigail Keam

CPSIA information can be obtained at www.ICGtesting.com
Printed in the USA
BVOW02s1659110116

432455BV00002B/69/P